I0831344

Other Edens

OTHER EDENS

DIPLODOCUS PRESS
Los Angeles • Bangkok
Main Office:
48, Sukhumvit Soi 33, Bangkok 10110, Thailand

ISBN 0-9771346-8-7 (hardcover)
ISBN 0-9771346-0-1 (trade paperback)

This book first appeared in a German translation as "Der Untergang von Eden" from Festa-Verlag, Germany.

This is the first English-language edition.
A trade paperback edition is also available, ISBN 0-9771346-0-1

Further information about the author may be found at
www.somtow.com
Further information about Diplodocus Press may be found at
www.diplodocuspress.com

10 9 8 7 6 5 4 3 2 1

Other Edens

Novellas of the Fall

S.P. SOMTOW

with an introduction by
William Hjortsberg

Los Angeles, Bangkok
DIPLODOCUS PRESS
2005

Contents

Ingres' Violin Introduction by William Hjortsberg ... *7*
A Different Eden ... 11
A Lap Dance with the Lobster Lady ... 43
Vanilla Blood ... 69
The Bird Catcher... 109
Beloved Disciple ... 137

Ingres' Violin ❧

An introduction to *Other Edens* by S. P. Somtow

by William Hjortsberg

The French have a wonderful expression, *le violon d'Ingres*, to describe an artist possessing talent in more than one discipline. This bon mot arose from the virtuoso violin-playing of the great 19th century painter, Jean Auguste Dominique Ingres. (One of Ingres' finest pencil portraits appropriately was of Paganini). Clinging tenaciously to a single gift, I regard the multi-talented with uncomprehending awe. S. P Somtow, the Thai-born writer of fantastic fiction, is a recent player on Ingres' violin. Under his given name, Somtow Papinian Sucharitkul, he is the artistic director of the Siam Philharmonic Orchestra and the Bangkok Opera, as well as a distinguished composer. As S.P. Somtow, he has produced more than forty books, ranging from the gothic, Vampire Junction, to his semi-autobiographical, Jasmine Nights. Along the way, Somtow earned nominations for many distinguished literary prizes, including the Hugo and Bram Stoker awards.

In *Other Edens*, Somtow's new collection of five stories, the Eton and Cambridge-educated writer fiddles up a varied medley of weird tales, each unique in tone and setting. "A Different Eden" recalls the work of Par Lagerqvist, who made such adroit use of the Christ legend in

Barrabas and The Sibyl, as well as D. H Lawrence's novella, "The Man Who Died," in its astute observation of the human nature of Jesus. Somtow provides a glimpse, through the eyes of the Savior's mother, of those mortal traits forever concealed by a presumed divinity.

The second story, "A Lap Dance with the Lobster Lady," jumps from philosophical fantasy to the ghastly comic-book world of Tales from the Crypt, where the sons of undertakers fall in love with freaks at seedy midnight carnivals and human organs replace automotive parts for macabre makeshift repair jobs. Later in the collection, Somtow acknowledges his debt to E. C. Comics. Like me, he was a fan back in the early 1950s of these imaginative short-lived publications where twenty-year-old geniuses like Wallace Wood and Jack Davis illustrated the bizarre tales of a young Ray Bradbury. Everyone exposed at puberty to E. C.'s brilliantly comic psychosexual graphic horror stories shares a common affinity for the darker netherworlds of fiction. If you like that sort of thing, you've got a date with the Lobster Lady.

"Vanilla Blood" taps into the common underlying vein of sexuality running just beneath the surface of all vampire tales. In this story, Somtow doesn't merely hint at the carnal aspects implicit in the lascivious bloodsucking popularized by such renowned nocturnal libertines as Dracula and Nosferatu, he revels orgiastically in their sanguinary passions. Told within the usually bloodless format of a courtroom transcript, the testimony of teenagers involved in a gruesome murder case burns with an erotic frenzy that might bring a blush to Anne Rice's jaded literary cheeks.

"Beloved Disciple," another story dealing with vampirism, takes a novel and delightfully blasphemous approach to this familiar genre. Imagine Jesus in his youth befriending a vampire he takes for an angel at a Druid burning man sacrifice in Cornwall. Who cannot but envy such a wild conceit? Somtow's vivid imagination leads the reader down some truly fantastic paths in this tale. The blood-sucking immortal instantly recognizes the profound spiritual nature of the Nazarene and when he meets him again, as a thirty-something preaching Messiah, becomes his reluctant disciple. What happens next is both shocking and hopefully profoundly troubling to anyone with a strict orthodox interpretation of Christianity. "Beloved Disciple" should be required reading for all the Bible-pounding fundamentalists presuming they alone know the truth.

My favorite story in the collection is "The Bird Catcher," which won a World Fantasy Award when first published. (It can also be found in *The Museum of Horror*, edited by Dennis Etchinson). This is not to say it is the best of the lot (such spurious comparisons are anathema to me) for I read them all with great pleasure. Yet, the masterful combination of a narrator recalling his youth, a sympathetic serial killer and an exotic locale drew me into the heart of the story like a violin cadenza seducing the listener, bringing new beauty to familiar forms. The skill with which Somtow evokes the perceptions of an eleven-year-old boy substantiates George Axelrod's enthusiasm when he dubbed the Thai author the "J. D. Salinger of Siam."

Visitors to S. P. Somtow's website will find a photo of him posing in the Bangkok Police Museum beside the mummified corpse of See Ui Sae Ung, the actual eater of children's livers, "the boogie man of Thailand," whom he wrote about in "The Bird Catcher." One can't help but admire such wry gallows humor.

Introductions at best should be brief as a handshake, a few quick words just as quickly forgotten to acquaint the reader with the storyteller making the true music. When he raises his baton for the downbeat, conductor Sucharitkul prepares to interpret the musical compositions of other artists, but when he sets pen to paper, S. P. Somtow holds the bow to Ingres' violin. Listen closely, for you are about to be serenaded by a master.

William Hjortsberg
Lion Head Cabin, Montana

A Different Eden❧

I am an old woman in Ephesus, sitting alone in a small house paid for by strangers. It is a small house, but it is real stone; I am an old woman, but they call me ageless; they call me mother to the world; they call me the daughter of the morning star; but I am just an old woman sitting alone in a small room, looking out over the alley, where the pilgrims jostle each other and are cheated by peddlers on their way to see the hundred-breasted goddess.

Years ago, in Jerusalem, while the pain was still fresh, a man named Paul came to see me. He was starting a new religion. He needed my endorsement; for in his pantheon I was to become the mother of God. He had crafted a new theology of such grandeur and such outrageousness that he believed it would sweep the world.

In vain, I told him true things about my childhood, and the birth of my son Joshua. I even broke terrible oaths of secrecy and revealed to him some of the mysteries that only women are allowed to know — I told him of the spring rites on the hillside, of the Roman centurion who might have embraced me in the guise of a horned god, of a secret flight to Egypt. But even this knowledge did not give him pause. He would keep telling me that the new religion was not one of literal truth, but of the truth concealed; that the truth he was fashioning was so much more true than this world of illusions we live in.

"The earth from which my perfect man, my Adam, is fashioned," he told me, "is a different dust; it's today's dust, you see, Hellenic and Roman and Judaean; my Adam will speak to people; I can sell him. I know about selling; I've sold tents."

I was not convinced. "My son was messiah of the month … and so were many others. He said many beautiful things. And now he has been dead a while, and the utterances have become the empty wind; some remember, some distort, some forget."

But Paul told me how he had seen my son in the clouds, in the lightning; my son would have been bemused at such an image of himself. I insisted that there was no magic here. Even then, I felt old, withered as the parched desert, drained of all feeling.

"Somewhere," Paul said, "there was magic."

"Where? Not in Nazareth, where they soon made mincemeat of my son's fanciful tales of a superhuman father. Not in Alexandria, where we lived like dogs, always hiding, always insecure; not in Cornwall, not in Galilee, not in Jerusalem, where they nailed him to the tree of death."

"You've left out something, Miriam."

"Perhaps there was a place of magic," I said, "but it wasn't even in the real world … the real hard world we know … the Roman world. It was beyond. Far beyond. Outside the known world, anything can happen; there are no rules. But now, as you see, we are back on earth."

"But you're wrong there. There's no rigid wall between paradise and the flesh. There was once, but it's leaking now. Anything is possible."

"It did not really happen. It was a dream."

"Who is to know that the world of dream is not reality, and reality but a shadow of the dream world?"

"Sophistry. You've been living with Greeks too long. Even your Aramaic has a twang to it."

Then again, hadn't my son lived with Greeks too long?

"All right," I said. "I'll tell you."

Why should it have surprised me? In Alexandria, we spoke Aramaic to my son; he answered us in Greek. Alexandria, a Greek city in an Egypt ruled by Rome, had its own kind of Jews; they considered themselves better than us. In Alexandria, even the Torah was in Greek, and those who sheltered us thought us uncouth for lapsing into the mother tongue. Joshua did not grow up with sights and sounds a proper Jew knew intimately: the screaming of a thousand lambs on holy days, the smell of their blood sluicing down the gutters of the Temple… the tramp of Roman boots on cobbled alleyways … the arhythmic thud-plop of a whore being stoned. We were always on the move, always being shown the door if we displeased someone; soon, I knew, we would run out of friends, or of friends of friends.

It was Joshua who was the problem. Now, as I sit out my last days in Ephesus, I hear rumors about his childhood … they are writing what they call "infancy gospels," fanciful anecdotes about his childhood. There's a story about him being teased by other children, killing them and resurrecting them for a lark … breathing life into clay pigeons, too. And irritating a schoolmaster by knowing too much. There's always a kernel of truth to the stories. For example —

When we were staying at the house of Samuel the Mapmaker, a client of Joseph's cousin the Arimathean, I came from the market to find Samuel's son David pinned to the floor of the atrium, and my son pummeling him in the face. I ran to him, pulled him away, but he writhed and punched at the air. David was unconscious.

"Let me go," Joshua screamed. I couldn't hold him even though he was just a child.

"What's wrong, what's the matter?"

"He told me my father's a Roman with antlers," he shouted. "He said I was spawned on a mountain top. He said that a demon raped you."

David lay motionless. And Joshua began to cry. Hysterically, appallingly. Then the doorway opened and I saw Samuel and my husband by the mezzuzah. And Joshua, just as abruptly, was dry-eyed, unrepentant.

David lay motionless on the mosaic stones, black and white, which spelled out words in Greek. Samuel ran to his son's side. David did not speak, and he stared unblinking at the patch of open sky. A fountain whispered; caged birds trilled.

"You've killed him," Samuel said to my son.

Joshua shook his head. "Not for long," he said. Wild-eyed, he left my side and knelt down beside the boy. "You can quit fooling now," he said. "Come back, come back from the dead."

Abruptly, David sat up. "You're a freak," he said softly. Pointed his finger in Joshua's face. Joshua backed away. Held out his hand for mine. Not to ask for solace, but to steady himself.

"Don't tell lies about my father," he said. His whisper hid an utter desolation, as though he were an angel cut off forever from the sight of God.

"I think," said Samuel, "that you people had better leave my house."

The boy was unmanageable. He was unruly. He made no friends, and so he found imaginary ones; he would stand in an atrium, talking to the wind, and he also had a habit of talking to statues of gods — Egyptian, Greek, Syriac, it didn't matter. If there was a shrine to Horus on a street corner, he'd strike up a conversation.

One day, my husband beat him for speaking to Priapus. Joshua was quite passive, did not cry out; that angered my husband all the more.

"There is only one god you are allowed to speak to, Joshua," he said when he was done. "You will remember that now."

"I'd speak to him if I could," Joshua said, "but he never shows his face to me. All the others do."

My husband wanted to go back to Judaea. "Look at your son," he would say. "He's gone pagan; half the time he runs around without any clothes on. When I teach him the Torah, he ignores me. One day he will have to become bar mitzvah, and I dread to think how he's going to botch that. He needs to be with proper Jews."

"You're consumed with guilt, Joseph, because you don't love him."

Joseph could not answer that, for he knew I could see through his posturing.

My son was only ten years old then; I told Joseph there was plenty of time. My husband was miserable in Alexandria, a severe man among hedonists, a learned man among dilettantes; and Joshua was heading toward trouble. There were gangs of idle youths in Alexandria. There were potent herbs to be smoked, wine to be drunk, and the Greeks believed that sex was little more than an itch to be scratched, which they did often, and with whatever person or creature was to hand.

My husband was not a modern man; he wanted nothing better than a woman of quiet modesty and an obedient son; he had neither of those things. Joshua was sullen, always angry. I wanted to much to tell him how special he was to me, how special his birth was, how even our fugitive status was born from his special quality; but I could not.

One night my husband and I argued until late. Joshua had not come home for supper. "I'm going to go look for him," said Joseph, "and in the morning we'll pack up, and leave for Nazareth."

"What about the danger?"

"Danger? it's been almost ten years."

"We shouldn't go back," I said. "Not unless there's a sign, a messenger."

"Messengers don't come to disobedient wives and wayward children," said Joseph.

"Only to the unbending, I suppose."

He raised his hand to me. I flinched. He stopped himself. He was not a cruel husband; I'll give him that; among the devout, wives are whipped for far less than impertinence.

"This is impossible," he said. "It's all wrong, everything is wrong. I'm a learned man among people who don't want to learn. This son of yours is recalcitrant. And you're not a dutiful wife."

It was an old argument. But that night I felt feistier than before; I wanted to argue back. "I'm as dutiful as can be expected," I said.

"Behind my back, you think of those women's rites. And the goddess who is abomination, whose statue stares down at us everywhere in this city. And the horned man in the hills." Which was a mystery of which no man should speak.

"No one forced you to marry me."

"You've given me no children," he said.

"In this place, Joseph?" I said. "In time. When we're home again, I'll give you sons."

"It's intolerable," he said. "This alien place … being shunted from stranger to stranger … and never knowing where Joshua is, whether he's talking to harlots or idol-worshippers or —"

"I'll find him," I said.

"In the night? Alone? A woman? In this iniquitous city?"

"I'm strong, Joseph," I reminded him. "Didn't I bear a child, without a midwife, in a cave? Didn't I walk with you to Egypt, with a child and our worldly possessions strapped to my back? If there's iniquity out there, I think I can resist."

"There's something that protects you. A demon, I think."

"Then my demon and I will go out into the street."

There was no demon. But there was a goddess.

I pushed my husband aside and went to find my son. It was not hard; my son loved to consort with the lowly. If it wasn't the alley of the lepers or the beggars' corner, it would be the street of the harlots, which ran from a Temple of Venus all the way to the wharf, where the drunken sailors prowled.

This was no Hellenic Aphrodite, coy and enigmatic, but the Babylonian Venus whom we call Ashtaroth, the earth that swallows up the sky's seed and spits forth life. In Judaea, the men worshipped the father whose name cannot be spoken; the women safeguarded more ancient truths; those truths, I fear, will die now that the Jews are scattered. I did not fear the Goddess; I was not afraid to walk along that street. Even the men who strutted and preened there were afraid. They do not want to acknowledge that before Eve, the obedient, there was Lilith, the elemental.

Joshua was a man-child who did not fear these women's brazen sexuality, and had no need to cast it to the ground and conquer it.

He was deep in conversation with one as I approached. They leaned against the temple walls, each one more painted than the next. The moonlight pierced the fronds of the date palms, and the women's faces were criss-crossed with shadow. The air sweated attar of roses; insects buzzed; clouds of incense billowed from braziers between the paws of stone sphinxes.

I couldn't help eavesdropping. The one he was talking to was a little one, perhaps no older than I was that night of the hillside rites of spring. She was telling him how sore she was, how she had bled, the pain she was feeling, "as if," she was saying, "I was a terracotta doll, broken, and no one knows how to mend me."

"Maybe I can," my son said. He looked her in the eyes; he had a look that said, I can draw your pain away. And he held her hands; not in arousal, but how you might hold the paw of a wounded animal. "I can't always mend things," he said, "but I'm getting better. One day I'll touch a person's hurt and just suck it into myself. And the pain will be gone."

"Is your father a doctor?" said the prostitute. "Usually these skills pass, you know, father to son."

"His father is a rabbi," I said, stepping from the shadows, "and a very frustrated one right now."

Joshua didn't look at me. He continued to hold the hands of the daughter of Lilith between his hands. Finally she said, "I think I'm feeling better now." And she broke away. It was too intense for her, perhaps. She ran off, and my son turned to look at me. But only for a moment; then he looked at the ground. I did not merit the soul-searching gaze that any common whore could receive from him.

Joshua of the penetrating stare, Joshua could to drain away a sick man's pain with a single glance ... this Joshua was not for me.

"Your father says it's time to go back. Time for you to take your Torah seriously; time to become bar mitzvah."

"He's not my father," Joshua said. "Besides, we've been waiting for a sign."

"You shouldn't be dictating to us; you're a child."

"I know, and you've let me run wild," he said; verbatim, one of the Carpenter's lectures. "You don't believe that." Sulking, he started to walk away. He was exasperating. Especially when he was right.

"Still, there's no sign, and we're out of time."

"There's been a sign. Today. An angel came." I noticed he had slipped into his Aramaic the Greek word for a messenger.

"What messenger?"

"You know him, mother." He turned to look at a small shrine to Caesar. A young Roman was wringing the neck of a pigeon to lay on the altar; another was sprinkling incense on the brazier; such common sights in Alexandria, scarcely worth noting; yet he watched, intent.

From the shadow of the temple wall a man emerged. Old. Sunken. Bearded. His white robe was in tatters; his skin was dark, and on his brow there was painted a scarlet curlicue, like a half-formed eye. It was his voice that was unmistakable; for he had a curious lilt, and his Greek was full of circumlocutions.

"You are knowing me, Miriam, I think," he said. And I remembered that we had called him Balthasar, because his true name was a tonguetwister in an alien language.

"But ..." I said . "Your silks, your jeweled turban...."

"Gone now, gone. But you know, I am having gained wisdom as I lost in sartorial preeminence."

"When you came to the cave, my child was just a baby. Some people called you a king."

"And some still may," he said. "But kings lead; I am a follower. I go where the stars lead me. And now, here I am. I have been sitting on a street corner, interpreting dreams and reading minds; parlor tricks really, waiting, waiting for a child on the brink of manhood, I child I once deemed worthy of frankincense."

"What do the stars want you to do with my child?" I asked him, for I knew he could only mean Joshua.

"My beautiful young prince," said the king, "ah, like me, you now resemble a pauper on the outside."

"Mother," Joshua said, "he says that in his kingdom there's an orchard where miracles happen."

It only occurred to me later that my son, who was stubborn about speaking Greek, had used a Hebrew word for orchard; he had called it "paradise."

"Mother, he wants me to go on a journey with him."

"So does your father," I said. "He wants to take us home."

"But I'm telling you, Mother, before I go home I'm going to find my real father."

And that, you see, was a Quest without a Golden Fleece; for I knew that he could never find a father who would satisfy him.

When I first moved into the house in Ephesus, I planted a tree in the middle of the little atrium garden. The tree was in memory of my son. I watered the tree with my tears. But the tree grew slowly....

I did not think my husband would countenance another journey, especially one whose destination we did not truly understand. But after our quarrel of the previous night, which had kept our hosts awake, it seemed as though we were about to be shunted to another family again; and so he acceded. We did not know how long the journey would be, or even whether it would be by land or sea.

"Perhaps," my husband told me, "this journey will heal us."

Joshua said nothing.

"Perhaps," my husband told him, "this journey, wherever it may take us, will throw you and me together long enough for us to read the Torah together, so that by the time you have to go to the Temple you will not make a complete fool of the Carpenter."

And again, Joshua said nothing.

But at dawn there came to the door a strange woman, veiled from head to toe in blue silk. She held a flute in her hand, and before my husband could ask her name, she held up the instrument, which seemed to play of its own accord. The melody was subtle; it twisted and turned; it was haunting, yet somehow you could not quite remember it from phrase to phrase. The woman's garment rustled though there was no breeze, and in the music of the flute you could hear the rushing of a mountain storm; I knew the sound well; it was the sound of my child being conceived, on the hill's side, in the high wind, in the circle of spring.

This is a vision, I told myself. I could see that my son and my husband did not see what I saw at all.

And when I looked a second time, she was gone; in her place was King Balthasar's charioteer, in full Indian battle raiment, his quiver on his back. And I knew that was all my husband saw.

But I had seen the Goddess. I knew it must be she. Men make a fuss about how men's secret wisdom must be hidden from women; but women are better at concealment. Most men have no notion that women have a secret cosmos, secret gods. My husband was such.

Though the woman's face was covered, she turned to me, and I felt that she must be smiling.

She did not speak, but merely pointed the way with her flute. Outside the door, there was a cart, covered with a woolen awning woven in fantastical designs such as the Persians love to devise. The Indian mage, still in his torn clothes, his hair still matted and filthy, bowed to us; he placed his palms together is a gesture of greeting.

We climbed into the cart; inside, it seemed far more capacious than it had on the outside. Woolen rugs canopied us and made walls; there seemed to be several chambers inside the vehicle.

Our host climbed up to greet us in his ornate Greek. "You will of course be forgiving of the humility of these surroundings; the stars bade me make haste; I could not summon an appropriate conveyance in time."

"And will you soon tell us where it is that the stars have asked you to take us?" Joseph said. "Some idea of how long we must travel would also suffice; and you know that we are Jews —"

"Who may not eat what others eat," the king said. "Do not be concerned, Joseph who is called the Carpenter. The place where we will go was built by Maya, the Lord of Illusion. You will eat and drink the empty air, and you will dance on the wind. The journey will take as long as it seems to take, yet it will be over in a single breath."

Joseph said softly, in the Ancient Tongue, "In thy sight, a thousand years is but as a single day."

My son sat up; it was if he had never heard the Psalms before.

My husband asked again, "But where is this place, this castle of illusion?"

And Balthasar answered, "Within."

And he opened the front-flap of the cart, and said to his charioteer, "Time to go."

I heard the flute music again. I heard the rushing of the wind. I felt the rumble of great wheels against the stone streets of the city. But we could not see outside. And presently our host retired to another chamber inside the vehicle, and my husband told me to absent myself, because it was time for him to teach the Torah to my son, and I should not be there lest I hear things that a woman should not know. So it was that I slipped out through the flap, and found myself sitting beside the driver, who was whipping the horses into a frenzy; the landscape flew by so quickly I could barely make it out; I saw great sphinxes, giant pyramids, oases, Cyclopean walls, ziggurats, and perfumed gardens; each time I blinked, another vista opened up.

I could hear my husband from within; when he recited the Torah, his voice had the resonance of a shofars and the pounding rhythm of a great drum.

He was speaking of the creation of the world, how the breath of God had but to touch the waters of chaos, and there was light; the words of the Torah thundered from him, and I was moved.

But then came my son's piping voice: "Father, I've heard that story in the marketplace. A tall man with a terraced beard recited it to me. The only thing that was different was the name of the creator: not Elohim, but a mother-thing named Nammu, and then Ki-An, and then Enlil."

Joseph said, "You are not to interrupt me. The Babylonians may also have such a story, but their is but the imperfect mirror of ours. We have the one true god; their god is like a fractured mirror; in the broken glass we can see many gods."

"But," Joshua said, "Elohim is plural. If it means God, why does it say 'the gods'? And if they can call Enlil and Nammu by name … why can't we?"

"God is all things at once," Joseph said. "Plural in singular, many in one, and that one unnameable, everything and nothing. Can't you see, it's just your imperfect command of the Old Tongue that confuses you?"

"Am I confused when I'm only pointing out that a word is plural?"

"Don't answer questions with questions."

The wind roared louder, and I could hear no more. But presently the charioteer turned to me, and it was no longer the charioteer but the woman I had seen earlier, veiled in blue. I said, "Do you think his real father would teach him differently?"

She said, "Do you mean the centurion?"

But she knew that I did not.

We passed through searing desert; at nightfall we reached an oasis ringed with palms. Camels were tethered, and there was a palace of tents; fires kept out the evening chill, and from within the tents came the sound of timbrels and psalteries and belled feet stamping. As we approached, the camels sank down on the sand, and a dozen painted girls emerged from the main entrance to the tent, prostrating themselves. More emerged; warriors, sages, musicians; all feel to the ground.

I naturally assumed that it was the Indian they were bowing to; but when I looked behind me, I saw that he too was on his knees. And it was Joshua, descending the rickety steps, who was receiving these people's obeisance. When Joseph emerged and saw, he was immediately in an ill humor.

"Tell these people to get up," he said to the king. "He must learn that we prostrate ourselves only to God."

"Indeed," said Balthasar, "he must learn it." Was there a hint of irony in his voice? He snapped his fingers, and the worshippers immediately rose to their feet and went about their business. "We will rest here awhile," he continued, "and refresh ourselves."

The tent-flap was pulled open; now the entire clearing was filled with raucous music. The floor was covered with the finest carpets, and as we entered, slaves washed our feet. The king motioned us to recline on great cushions stitched from old kilims and stuffed with rose-leaves; so as not to intrude on the men, I sat further off, next to the ensemble of musicians, all female, all veiled. Slaves poured tea from tall bronze vessels with serpentine spouts. Though there were elaborately dressed dignitaries present, I had the feeling that this entire place had been conjured up for our eyes alone, a particularly vivid mirage.

Balthasar said to Joshua: "So, what did Joseph teach you on your way to this place?"

"He was telling me about the creation of the world," my son said, "but there were things that didn't sound right."

"My son's mind is like a fishnet," Joseph said, "and he has snared creatures with claws and tentacles along with the fish with scales and fins that are our proper diet."

"We will tell you another story tonight," said the king.

And I saw that the woman in blue was standing amidst the orchestra, holding her flute aloft, and from an inner chamber of the tent there came twenty-two dancers. Their eyes were kohled, their hair in delicate black ringlets; they wore veils and their ankles were bound with bells. Their veils fluttered as they moved.

The music grew louder; the drums pounded in the rhythm of an agitated heart, and the plucking and piping became frenzied. I watched my husband. He was entranced ... who would not be? ... aroused. He drank deeply of the proffered wine, the wine-jugs cooled in a mound of packed snow that must have been brought from a thousand miles away.

The dancers were beautiful. They leaped; as their veils shifted, I could see the taut musculature of their thighs ... there was something almost manly about them ... their eyes darted, quivered, circled in a synchronized choreography as elaborate as the dance itself. And I realized that they exuded a sexual power ... that it touched me ... it was their maleness that affected me, even as their feminine qualities had stirred my husband.

Now there were cymbals and timbrels, harps and lutes, and panpipes and flutes wailed above the clanging. The veils were flying, weaving patterns in the flickering firelight. You could see more flesh. The dancers moved with such precision they seemed like cogs in one of those Roman mechanical marvels, those contraptions that keep their public baths flowing or their catapults wound up. They climbed over each other, fell apart, reassembled their bodies into writhing creatures with many arms and legs. The audience, was enraptured; they did not move; they seemed, indeed, to have fallen quite motionless; it occurred to me once more that they were not entirely human, but put there only to make this vision more complete.

The music swelled; there was a shuddering climax as all the dancers mounted one another to form a whirling, precarious human rope; then, it seemed, they climbed up a ladder made entirely of themselves, while the shortest dancer, a child perhaps, twirled on his toes on the head of the dancer beneath. It was dizzying; it was ingenious; and then, with the music so cacophonous that it could no longer be called music, it was over; the rope tumbled to the ground and the dancers were in a heap, and the veils, tied end to end, were being whisked into the ceiling by an assistant hanging from the tent-poles.

They were near-naked now, these twenty-two men … or were they women? Their breasts were so tightly bound with a flesh-colored cloth that one could not tell, and for the parts below, a loincloth of the same hue was wrapped so cunningly that one could see no telltale outline of gender.

A gong sounded, and the dancers melted into the shadows. The feast continued into the night; I retired to the women's quarters, and thence to the chamber they had apportioned to my family, to find that a pallet of sheepskins had been spread out for me. A bondswoman was folding clothes and putting them away in a carved cedar chest.

In the distance, a harpist played, and sang some saga in a long-dead tongue. Again the voice seemed neither man nor woman.

"Woman, do you know —"

The slave turned to me. Her face was veiled, but her very gaze perfumed the air. "Yes," she said, "I do know."

"Were they men or women?"

"Neither, my lady. They belong to a caste of sacred man-women; they may originate as men or women, but they take great pains to fashion themselves into something in between."

"Why?" I asked.

She held up bronze mirror and began to comb my hair. I had rarely been so pampered, and I allowed myself to luxuriate.

"But you already know why," she said, and I knew her voice at that moment, and I was honored — and afraid — because a supernatural being was acting like my slave. "They seek to emulate the perfect state of humankind, before there were men and women, before the war between the sexes."

It was true. I'd realized the answer before she even spoke. I wanted to question her more, but she vanished in a flurry of glittering dust. And so I prepared to sleep, and waited. And heard voices outside the door-flap. My son was arguing with my husband. Their voices were shrill, and the substance of their argument esoteric. "Abomination, abomination," my husband was shouting, and my son was speaking of how Adam was, perhaps, at his creation, a hermaphrodite, since his femininity had not yet been extracted from his side and breathed into a second handful of dust.

When they came in, they must have realized I had overheard some of their arguing. Because the things they spoke of were not for women to hear, they stopped, and looked at each other, and looked away; in the sooty glow of the chamber's one oil lamp, their faces held a sullen menace.

"I was right," Joseph said to me. "This trip is bringing me closer to my son; we argue now; before, we never spoke at all."

Joshua did not speak until my husband was asleep and snoring. When he was sure Joseph would not wake up — what with the wine and the dancing girls — he said to me, "Walk with me a while, Mother."

The night and I were young, and my husband was an old man, crotchety, dogmatic; I wanted to breathe the desert air, so I went with my son. The guards at the door of the tent-palace were the same holy transvestites who had danced for us. They made obeisance to us, their palms held together, inclining their necks.

In the moonlight, my son said, "Why is he so angry all the time?"

"Because you won't treat him as your father," I said.

"But he's not," he said.

"At least he's trying to be," I said.

"He's a strange man," Joshua said. "He knows so many facts, and yet he only wants to put them together one way."

"He doesn't mean to be cold to you," I said. "It's just that —"

"I'm a bastard," Joshua said. "I wish you'd stop lying to me about the special circumstances of my birth, about angels and portents and wise men's gifts —"

"But one wise man came back," I said. "And you were the one who called him an angel."

"Joseph says he's a messenger from the dark goddess whom women worship in secret."

"But he agreed to come on this journey."

"Because he doesn't want to know that he's afraid. But I do know. He's an open book. More open to me than his Torah, anyway."

And though he was the one who invited me to walk with him, he sped up and moved away from the encampment, in the direction of the desert. In the distance, there were dunes, stark in the moonlight, slowly shifting, sifting in the chill wind.

I caught up with him. "Joshua —" I said. I put my hand on his shoulder. But he brushed me away.

"Maybe if I stand out here long enough," he whispered, "my father will come and talk to me."

"Joseph's asleep," I said.

"Yes," Joshua said, "he is." And he turned from me, and walked further into the expanse of sand, his gaze fixed on the moon.

"You'll catch cold," I said, but I knew he wasn't listening anymore.

The tree in my atrium in Ephesus has ten branches. I've kept it very carefully pruned, so the branches are evenly spaced and the foliage has room to spread out. It's the only thing that lives in that atrium garden; everything else I've planted always dies, so I've taken to letting the stonemasons dump their failed statues here; there's a few Cupids, one of Jupiter, and many abortive Dianas of Ephesus, with her many breasts, she is tough to get right.

Sometimes one of the Christianoi will come and see me; Paul's propaganda war to make my son into God seems to be working; I've heard them whisper to each other, "Look, look, God's mother." And they tell me the tree symbolizes the crucifixion, and they exclaim, "Lo! the tree flourishes, and all around it the statues of the ancient gods have been smashed; our new order is sweeping away the old." They do not know, of course, that no one smashed those statues, least of all some supernatural power; these gods were never killed, because they were never born; they are trapped in half-formed stone for all eternity.

One day that tree will be full-grown, and the ten branches will be ladder to the bosom of God.

At least, that's what they have told me.

This was a journey of the spirit. I cannot tell how much time passed, or if time passed at all. On the second day, the sound of my husband instructing my wayward son was quickly wearying, and I crawled out to the front once more to sit beside the charioteer who was to me the goddess. I smelled the sea as soon as I emerged. The sun was bright; the wind had a briny moisture to it.

I had stepped out onto the deck of a ship, but such a vessel as I had never seen on the Sea of Galilee. Where the horses had been, there were wave-crests like row after row of white-maned steeds. Beneath us, I could hear the drumbeat of a hortator, and I could he the rhythmic slap of the oars against the ocean. The prow of the ship was a many-breasted woman with blue skin; although she was made of wood, her eyes were living; I knew now that the vessel, like the horse-drawn cart, was an extension of the goddess's body.

A servant brought me a tray of fruit. Like the musicians and the dancers in the oasis, this slave seemed both male and female.

There were pomegranates, figs, and quinces; grapes, dates, and apples. The servant kneeled before me, holding out the platter; I reached out to touch the fruit, and then I thought again.

The pomegranate is the fruit of the dead; the secret wisdom of the women has taught me that the leaves and the seeds of the pomegranate are what binds the souls of the dead to the world beneath. And I thought too of the quince, which some claimed was the fruit of the knowledge of good and evil. I wondered if the other fruits had darker meanings, too.

"Is this fruit forbidden?" I asked the servant.

She only said, "Nothing is forbidden, my lady, unless you yourself forbid it."

At that moment, I saw King Balthasar emerge from below decks. He saw me and said to me, "Remember, Miriam, you are being a traveler in the realm of Maya now; nothing is real."

I still did not feel I should eat the fruit.

"You're going to see terrible things now," he went on. "But remember … it's illusion."

Even as he spoke, I saw my son and husband in an animated conversation some distance away, leaning over the side of the ship. Halfway to the horizon, two whales were breaching the waves, the sun glancing off the slick skin. They were coupling. I had never seen whales in the throes of passion before; the one lay on her back, the other mounted her, and the pair swimming at top speed to sustain the stability of the position.…

And far away, against the horizon, there were jagged boulders, a blue-green mist, the vaguest outline of land.…

Out of nowhere, a storm unleashed itself. Rain pelted down. There was thunder and lightning, and the androgynous crew members were rushing about, scrambling to get below deck. I had no time to think. The ship heaved, I staggered, my stomach churned … I feel to the deck. Brine sluiced the planks. Salt flooded my nostrils. I was spluttering. Trying to grab hold of anything. I could see treasure chests floating into the sea … silks and jeweled goblets bobbing up and down and … the wet wind lashed at us. The ship righted itself, and I heard shouts of: "The Carpenter … he's fallen overboard …"

The storm was already subsiding, harsh sunlight bursting through chinks in the cloud cover. The crew were climbing back up now, tying things down, staring at the ocean ... and as I rushed to towards the stern I could see my husband in the water, furiously trying to swim toward a plank....

And there was my son. "Don't worry, Mother," he said. "I'll bring him back." And he smiled at me, a smile of such utter calm that it chilled me. Because though the wind was dying, the waters were still turbulent, and the sailors still in panic over a tempest that had lasted but a moment.

How could Joshua bring him back? Joseph was being carried out further to sea. And the seamen were throwing down ropes, but no one wanted to leap in after him.

Except my son. He stripped off his Grecian chiton and his head covering, and leaped naked into the sea. I had never seen my son swim before. In Alexandria, he had stuck to the streets, not the sea. But even now, he did not swim.

He fell very slowly, as though riding the wind.

He landed on his feet on the waves.

And I thought, *He will not suffer thy foot to be moved....*

With great deliberation, carefully placing one foot before the other, like a temple dancer on a tightrope, he moved towards his stepfather.

I heard others whispering, "He's walking on water."

But I could see, just below the surface, the dark, unmoving outline of leviathan. The sea water sparkled in the sun; his bright eyes shone against his olive complexion; he seemed as strong as fullgrown man as he pulled his stepfather from the ocean.

The crew were gathering now, and someone cast down a rope ladder; and it seemed that on the instant that Joshua and my husband alighted on the ladder, the monster of the deep sounded, and a moment later the pair of whales was to be seen afar off, and a strange music filled the air, keening and thrumming at the same time; it was, Balthasar assured me, a song the whales sang often, and always to the glory of God.

A few moments passed; Joseph looked at Joshua as a sailor threw a garment over his shoulders.

At length, my husband said, "Well, at least you're dressed like a Jew now."

"I'm trying to please you," Joshua said.

Joseph said, "Then don't walk on water; you'll catch your death."

"I didn't walk on water," Joshua said. But I knew that the others had all witnessed a miracle; only I had seen how the monster of the deep had interrupted his lovemaking so that my son would not dash his foot against the sea.

"And don't argue with me anymore. There's a time for debating, and a time for listening."

"I'm listening."

And I saw, then, that though neither of them could speak of it, there was a kind of love between the two of them. I did not think they would ever come to admit it. They would not even look at each other.

And now, almost tripping over the robe that was far too long for him, Joshua turned to me; wordlessly, still wet and shivering, he fell into my mother embrace; but even close to me he was wary, unyielding.

And suddenly we came upon those shoals that I had seen at the very edge of the horizon, and King Balthasar was urging us inside.

"I don't need to go in," Joshua said. "I'm not afraid."

"Go in anyway," said the king. "We're about to be shipwrecked."

The ship foundered on a massive rock, and I heard a groan as of splintering timber, but with a curiously human quality to it....

At this point in my narrative, the man who was about to create a new religion on my son's dead bones broke in. "You don't have to go on," Paul, Saul, whatever his name was, said to me. "I've heard enough. There's nothing I really need in what you're telling me."

I smiled. "Ah, but there is," I said. "It's all there, every bit of pagan symbolism you need to make your religion palatable to the Gentiles."

He paused then, because he knew I had seen through him. He wanted a story from me that he could spin into a perfect arc of godhead, with the bitter widow as golden Isis suckling the crucified rebel as shining Horus; me as the Great Mother ploughing the blood of my son and lover into the soil to bring forth the harvest; he wanted to ship me off to Ephesus to replace the hundred-breasted huntress. Which, in the end, came to pass.

Paul said, "I want something more powerful than reality ... I want truth."

The kind of distinction the Greeks love to make, and which quite staggers those of us who speak less dissembling tongues.

The beach we foundered on was India. Not the India of history, where Alexander the Great had stumbled upon the far boundary of the universe, and turned back from the edge to encounter only drunkenness and death; this was, perhaps, an India of the mind. Though Paul would no doubt draw many comparisons to Alexander; for Alexander, too, was a god's son, a messiah of sorts, dead in his thirties.

From the impact of the ship against the rocks to the time we stepped onto the sand was mere moments. It seemed to me that the ship fell apart in two halves, and the halves dematerialized into the burning air, and there had never been a ship at all. Instead, there was a white elephant, caparisoned in cloth of gold; atop its back was a howdah cunningly carved of wood, with caryatid columns and a roof made from the images of many-headed demons.

The elephant knelt, and the king led the way, mountain by way of gilt steps that were wheeled up to the creature's side by attendants.

Seated on the elephant's neck was the woman in blue.

"Your journey will soon be over, Joshua," the king said to my son, who, since his adventure with the sea, was ever more withdrawn, huddling in a corner of the howdah, hugging his knees and staring at the ground as it swayed beneath us. "Look, Miriam; do you see the castle?"

I saw only snowcapped mountains, impossibly tall, impossibly far.

"No, you don't see it yet," said the king. "You see only the Himavant, and high Kailasa, dwelling place of the gods. Open your mind, Miriam … let the illusions in."

The elephant was climbing a steep path, pausing now and then to roll a fallen tree trunk out of its way. We traveled for what might have been days; time was a flexible thing in these countries past the known world's edge.

The mountain still seemed impossibly far. We stopped at a waystation in a clearing. Sandalwood incense filled the air, and there was a temple in the same ornate style as the elephant's howdah. Priests in white robes and turbans wandered haughtily about. There was a statue of a goddess with a hundred arms, wearing a necklace of skulls, her feet trampling on corpses.

"There's your demon Ashtaroth," Joseph said to me. "The man-killing she-beast. It seems that she rules here."

I did not argue with him; I knew it would be useless. I gazed at the statue. I knew that the goddess had a thousand names; she was Persephone, queen of darkness; she was the mother of the spirits that visit men in the night and drain away their seed; she was Lilith; she was the goddess who had been the consort of the most high once, and who was now condemned to rule over dirt and shadows; in this country, at least, men acknowledged her power.

We resumed our journey at dawn. The road grew wilder. We passed a surging river lined with temples; men and women bathed in its waters, and the dead were burned in pyres there, their ashes cast onto the waters. We passed ascetics, naked old men covered with filth, some standing on one leg, some with their cheeks and torsos pierced with metal rods, all bone thin; we passed some sitting cross-legged under trees, their eyes closed, gazing as it were upon some inner vision; we saw men whirling themselves into frenzies, women dancing among monkeys; we saw men prostrating themselves before oxen, and everywhere the many-armed demons, towering over shrines, guarding palace gates, painted on walls; and always the lady in blue drove the white elephant forward, tapping its neck with a silver goad.

"This is a desolate place," my husband said. "Abomination everywhere. Men who imitate women, men who worship beasts. I thought Alexandria was a second Sodom, but this is beyond imagination."

Joshua was still huddled in the corner of the howdah, staring at emptiness.

"Look at what it's done to our son," Joseph said. "This journey is killing him, filling him with terrible ideas, destroying his soul."

And I marveled, not only at what he said, but that this was the first time he had said our son; and I knew there was a kind of magic at work.

So I simply said, "We'll be home soon."

I think my husband would have embraced me if we were not in a small open chamber perched on a lumbering beast. I put my hand out to steady myself; he held onto it, and, perhaps, squeezed it; I was not sure. I thought: He does love me, underneath it all, though I've put him through so much. I wanted to put my arms around him, but I knew he would think it immodest of me.

We stopped again. This new encampment was a place shrouded in mist; moisture seeped into our lungs; scarred rocks emerged from the roiling fog, and here and there a shrine stood, its offerings mouldy and half devoured by wild animals. The mountains were still just as far away as before.

We took shelter in a cave. But it was nothing like the cave in which I held my newborn child. This cave was covered with murals depicting the exploits of strange gods. Gold leaf was peeling from wooden beams; the scent of incense was everywhere; and there were statues of a man, cross-legged, his hair aflame; whose eyes held a rare serenity. And then, in niches in the cave, there were live men too, anchorites I guessed, in the same cross-legged attitude. Their eyes were closed. Like many we had seen on the road here, they seemed to be gazing inward.

"Who are these men?" I asked the king.

"They believe that the world is an illusion," he said. "They are trying to end that illusion. They are thinking that if they are perfectly still, they will touch the still center of the cosmos, and when they have become as nothing, they will be everything."

There were bats and monkeys in the cave, too; the bats perched high up, sleeping, like black furry roof-tiles; the monkeys scurrying, peering, chattering, stealing the offerings to the gods.

Balthasar took his place upon a throne of rock, with incense braziers at his feet. Vassals brought food; other servants spread out pallets of straw for us in shadowed crannies of the cave. Joshua seemed at last to have become impatient. He wasn't in a corner rocking himself back and forth now. He was pacing. Finally he asked the king about his father. "Who is my father, then? Why did he send you to me? Why is it taking so long to reach him?"

The king said only, "You will be reaching him, Joshua, when your soul will tell you you are willing to reach him."

"Riddles! You're as bad as Joseph. You told me there would be an orchard at the end of this journey. You told me my father would be waiting for me, and I would finally know who I am."

"No riddles, my beautiful young prince. You do not know the answers because you do not want to know them."

And in the night, with the moonlight streaming in through high fissures in the cavern's roof, I could not sleep; and I saw that neither my son nor my husband were sleeping either. I lit an oil lamp and wandered listlessly; the cave was labyrinthine.

In the hollow where the king dozed on his capacious throne, the walls were painted from floor to ceiling. These were the gods and demons these people believed in; each one had many heads and arms. A great ape yawned the moon and the stars. A goddess dancing across the clouds wielded the lightning. And directly behind the throne, there was painted a golden door, and on either side of the door were depicted Greek letters — alpha on the left, omega on the right. It did not surprise me that there was Greek here; perhaps the murals had been painted in the days when Alexander the Great ruled all the world.

Next to the door was depicted a golden chariot, even in the light of my flickering oil lamp it seemed to shine of its own. Next to the chariot stood a god, his skin completely blue, holding a flute. His face was the essence of manliness, yet it held a feminine beauty as well. His eyes sparkled. I found myself staring at that face; for it was a face I seemed to recognize, though I could not imagine whence.

Presently I heard voices; it was Joseph and Joshua deep in conversation yet again; I could hear the stark music of the ancient tongue, and I knew that Joseph was making another attempt to teach my son the meaning of the Torah. Because I knew that my husband would find it unseemly, I ducked behind the throne, pressed myself against the stone, tried to will myself into invisibility.

Joseph was speaking of the first words of the Torah. "Every word, every letter," he told Joshua, "encapsulates a myriad hidden meanings. For example, we say in Aramaic that in the beginning God created heaven and earth; but does the text really say that? No — the word *bara*, 'created,' comes second, not third, do you see that? God could be the object as easily as the subject. So what created God? Surely only God can have created God. And then the word et, the accusative particle that precedes the words for heaven and earth — how is that written but as *aleph* and *I*, the beginning and ending of the alphabet, which by extension means the entire alphabet, the key to all creation?"

Joshua said, "But what about the question I asked before? About how the text doesn't really say 'God' at all, but 'the gods'?"

"God is an axiom. You can't argue with an axiom."

"But when God said, 'You shall have no other gods before me,' he didn't say that other gods don't exist."

"Demons," said Joseph. I saw his shadow in the lamplight, huge and not unlike a demon itself. Joseph turned a corner. And saw me. "Miriam!" he gasped. "You know you can't listen to men's talk."

Fury welled up inside me. I thought of the torment of childbirth, the dickering between Joseph and my parents over my soiled chastity, the trek across the desert with my baby on my back … "Your thousand interpretations of the meaning of those words," I said. "I know one that you haven't thought of."

Joseph looked at me as if to say, "How could a woman understand?" But he didn't say it out loud. He stood there, in front of the painted doorway, challenging me.

"The word *bara* has no gender," I said. "And the world *elohim* might be plural. What if the real meaning was, 'In the beginning, she created the gods?"

"Blasphemy!" my husband scoffed. "That's bound to happen when a woman meddles in the affairs of men."

But Joshua said, "Don't speak to my mother that way," and ran at him full tilt with his fists out.

"Don't hit your father!" I shouted.

"He's not my father!" Joshua screamed at the top of his lungs. He started pummeling at Joseph with his fists. He was hysterical, lashing out, punching the air. My husband stepped aside and Joshua was banging at the painted portal and the plaster was flaking away and —

There was a crack as of smashing wood. Joshua's fists broke through the wall and all at once he was sucked into the mural … I screamed … the wall closed up around him and —

He was gone.

And so was the image of the golden chariot and the charioteer.

My son — flesh and blood — absorbed into an illusion — and yet it had the logic of a vivid dream — and I was not afraid. It seemed to me as it should have been. I heard, from within the rock, a muffled laughter … the happy laughter of a child … something I had not heard in the real world for many years.

"This is too much," Joseph cried, and he began pounding on the painted door with his fists. I thought I heard the hollow resonance of old wood, but nothing gave way. I went up to the wall. Put my finger on it. It was flat, but I definitely touched the texture of wood; I tingled. A glow seemed to emanated from the door and envelop me in a cold blue light.

My husband stepped back. "Have I married a witch?" he whispered. And quoted the words of scripture: "Thou shalt not suffer a witch to live."

"Don't kill me, Joseph," I said softly. "I don't know what is happening. I don't understand anything."

"Your demon-goddess is manipulating you," he said. "Even if you don't know what you're doing … you're her puppet."

It was at that moment that the room filled with light, as though a thousand torches had been lit. I turned. There were the hermaphrodite servants of the king, and each one held aloft a flaming sword. As though for the first time, I saw the cavern whole, with niche after niche of anchorites in deepest meditation; they were all awakening now, yawning, stretching their limbs as though they had been in a millennial sleep. And there was the king himself; he had stepped down from the throne, and stood between me and my husband, no longer clothed in the tatters of an ascetic, but in the full splendor of his kingship, his hair topped by a jewel-encrusted turban, his robes of peacock-hued silk, a pectoral jewel like a massive diamond eye.

"Where have you taken my son?" Joseph shouted.

Balthasar smiled. "I took him nowhere," he said. "This was always his journey, not mine; I am but a messenger. You may follow him, if your heart is steady and your will is sure."

"I can go anywhere he goes," he said. "I raised him, I taught him right from wrong; he belongs to me even if not in the flesh."

"Then go to him," said the king.

As Joseph turned to the door, I saw that the Greek letters had burst into flame, and the lines of fire were transforming themselves into Hebrew: and the Alpha was twisting itself into א just as the Omega was becoming ת. But the door would not yield to him. He banged until I could see the blood oozing from his clenched fists, and yet the stone did not give, though now and then there was a telltale creak, as though the fabric of reality were willing itself to shift but was not quite able to.

"Joseph, Joseph," said the king, "you are in a cage that you have been making of your own accord. You must let go your conscious self. If the Torah is a great edifice, you have given it brick by brick to your wife's son, and each brick you have illuminated with skill and even passion; yet a temple is not wrought from bricks, but from the soul."

And it was then that my husband wept. He had never wept in my presence before. He wept, I think, because he knew every word of the Torah, yet he did not know the word that could open one child's heart.

"Miriam," said the king to me, "do you want to know who Joshua's father is?"

"No," I said firmly. And so saying, I consigned to the abyss my memory of the masked man with the antlers, the handsome centurion named for a were-leopard of the night, and all that spring ritual on the hillside.

As soon as I said no, the letters began to glow again, and this time they metamorphosed into blue bolts of lightning that formed an even more ancient script, thus: 𐤀 and 𐤕. And I knew them for letters that people had used a thousand years before ... the people of the Great Goddess, who had occupied the promised land before the coming of my people. They were the first and last letters of the Phoenician alphabet. And so there were three magics at play: the magic of earth, of the past, of the mother, my magic; the magic of the Greeks, whose civilization would influence the future; and the here and now, the eternal present, Joseph's magic.

The past and the future could enter the gateway; the present could not. And I understood why: Joseph's kind had already been driven from Eden. My kind had remained there, had never truly entered the world. And Joshua's kind had yet to be.

There were three Edens behind that door. Three choices. Three human conditions.

If I stepped through it, I would not see what Joshua saw.

King Balthasar said, "You and your husband, Miriam, were not invited to this feast. But Miriam, as you are a woman, and as you are all women, and as you are the woman beneath the sky, she whom the rain makes fertile and who brings forth all the good things in the world, you may if you open your inner eye see all three Edens."

I put my husband's hand in mine.

I saw: a creature both man and woman, split in twain, the two halves always seeking each other out; I saw passion. I saw the man and the woman making love in the orchard. I was the man and I was the woman. His penis was the sword of flame. His arms were the enfolding branches of a great tree that encircled the world. He leaped out of my body as leviathan breaching the deep.

My lips were the fruit of knowledge. My hips were the gates of desire. My eyes were the stars, and my hair the nurturing night.

My husband groaned as I clenched him hard inside me, and the waters that flowed from every opening in my body were the waters of creation, the waters on whose face God breathed; and my husband loved me for six days, six eternities in the mind of the almighty; and on the seventh day, he stared into my eyes as he held me, and his gaze held a terrible despair, the despair that all men feel when they have conquered what their heart has always desired … for all men, after the explosion of pleasure and contentment, soon begin to sense an unease, a feeling of "Why was there not more?"

And with that single look, I understood why Joseph could not return to Eden.

Man who is born already possessing the perfection of what could be possessed will still ask "Why is there not more?"

That was why he had been driven from Eden … or rather he had caused himself to be driven from Eden … because it is human to quest for the ever-unreachable, to reach for the ever-untouchable. To taste paradise, yet never be allowed to return — this was the source of all man's creativity, man's genius. I understood my husband now; I understood men.

If he returned to paradise, he would no longer be human.

The vision faded; I sat with my back to the garden door, my husband sleeping in my arms, smiling, content, it seemed, for the first time since we had left Nazareth.

And so I rose, and left my husband sleeping; and the king, who could not himself enter, held open for me the gateway to my Eden.

Immediately, a wind caught me. It carried me above the clouds; I saw the world spinning below, saw moons and stars whirl over me; I was riding some kind of chariot through the sky, and the goddess stood before me, whipping the steeds into a frenzy, before I could catch my breath, I was dropped down on a hillside in Nazareth, the place of the women's rites. It was night. I knew the place. I had arrived at a moment in my own past. I was so young then … it was not long after my first bleeding. But inside my own mind, I was also an older woman, seeing with the eyes of experience … I was seeing the time of my innocence with the hindsight of having already tasted the fruit from the tree of knowledge….

Dancing in the dark. The stars wheeled overhead. The moon wept blood. On this hillside, we women chanted and banged our drums and spoke in a secret language men cannot know. Our song was as ancient as the hills; these trees and boulders had heard this music in a time before there were Jews in Judaea.

Within the circle of women there stands a creature, a man, I think, a man or a tree. His face is masked in foliage. A deer's antlers sprout from his forehead. His arms are spread out, cruciform. As the mist roils across the stony ground, I find myself being drawn toward him … reeled in, almost, like a fish from the sea … and I see the man's eyes … my eyes. He embraces me. He laughs. My laugh. He hugs me hard in his arms, his arms sinewy and sinuous; his arms are the branches of a great tree, they are serpents, constrictors, they are flaming clouds; he sucks me into his embrace … I cry out … for as my lips seek out his lips, as we stand locked in a sensual coupling, I know those eyes at last … the eyes that have looked away all these years … the eyes that would never meet mine, though they gazed freely at the lowliest beggar … my son has come to me as a raging firestorm from the sky … my son has planted himself within me … yet this is no abomination … there is no incest when a god engenders himself.

And my son divides me in two. I am like the Red Sea; I am a channel for the chariot of fire to race skyward.

At the center of the orchard there is a tree whose roots penetrate deep into the heart of darkness, and whose topmost branches caress the very face of God.

The chariot disappears into the face of the sun. I am alone.

A terrible sadness comes over me; it is the sadness a woman feels after childbirth. But soon, I know, my spirits will soar. I will come down from the mountain all alone, but I will always know now that I don't need a man to complete me. The wind was chill, but soon the sunlight will warm the air, and I dance. I am woman. I am the world.

In the third vision, I am the woman in the serpent. The serpent has wrapped itself around the tree of life. The serpent has one hundred breasts, and from each breast there pours a river. Is this how my son sees me? As the dragon who guards the great mystery of his birth? I do not have time to ask myself more questions, because my son has come into the orchard. His charioteer is an angel with blue skin, clothed in the sun.

My son leaps from the chariot. His sword is forged from the tears of the stars. There is the tree; from every branch hang fruits … fruits like jewels, like scrolls, like trumpets. I must protect the treasure. No one can steal the golden apples of the gods.

My son charges towards me, sword outstretched. From the heavens comes the music of seven shofars, and the branches of the tree are lashed together with liquid lines of light.

I am the dragon. I must protect the treasure.

"Why have you come?" I try to speak gently, as a mother, but from my throat there issues a draconian roar; the earth itself rumbles at my footfall; sulphurous flames belch from my throat.

"I've got to kill you," says Joshua. "Can't you see that? I don't want to, but it's destiny."

"But I'm your mother," I say, and I slither forward to embrace him in my scaly arms, I offer him sustenance from my hundred breasts, but he plunges the sword into me. Over and over and over, until I am bleeding in a hundred places, and the rivers that run from my breasts run red.

Blood fountains up. It is more crimson than polished rubies. The wounds are burning. It touches the sky. The blood turns to air. I am dissolving into nothingness.

"You are my mother," says Joshua, "and I won't forget how much you loved me. But it was written that I would slay the dragon darkness, and climb to the top of the tree, and gaze upon my father face to face."

I try to cling to him, but I am melding with the rays of the sun, the emanations that stream from the tree of life. I am dying, I think, but in the midst of dying I realize that I am becoming one with everything; I am the air, the tree, the earth, the sun; I am knowledge; I am death.

I see the charioteer now. He is a giant. His name is Krishna. He is but a fragment of God, even as I, the slain darkness, was another piece of divinity. He stretches out his hand to hold the tree steady.

Because I am the air, my son is breathing me into his lungs. Because I am the sun, I warm him. The charioteer gives my son a leg up. My son springs skyward, branch to branch, climbing hand to hand on the twenty-two filaments of light that link the branches; up there, at the summit, he will pierce the canopy of clouds, he will see God.

My son lay sleeping for many days in the palace of King Balthasar. I tended him. The king assembled provender and made arrangements for our return. After a day, Joseph too began to help me, squeezing a rag dipped in snow-cooled water on my son's forehead, touching him gently, realizing for the first time how precious he was to him.

I was away from Joshua's side when he awakened. I was sitting at a window (for Balthasar's palace was many stories high, and perched on a mountain ledge) watching dancers with gold and purple saris swaying to the sound of flute and drum.

As I watched, I noticed the mist clearing … the mist that had draped the palace since our arrival … and I saw for the first time how green the valley below was, how emerald-clear; I saw the king's city straddling the mountain side, with stately columns, an agora, domes and gardens and fountains and statues.

Joshua was mumbling something. I turned. Joshua said, "Father." And he put his arms around my husband's neck, and Joseph hugged him, I think for the first time; he hugged him and he wept. It was not a moment for me to intrude; I stayed out of sight, as a mindful woman should; but like all women, I saw more clearly, saw what they don't see.

Joseph did not say, This is the first time you have called me father. But he knew it, and it melted his hard heart.

Joshua did not say, I am giving myself to you of my own free will, knowing that one day I must face another destiny; we all have roles to play in a vast cosmic drama, but for now, I want to be a child, I want to be loved as a child, made much of; it will be over all too soon.

But his silence said all those things, if only my husband would listen.

Joseph said, "Let's go home now."

Joshua said, "I've climbed to the top of the tree of life, and I've seen what is there … it's nothing, Father."

Wasn't that what the anchorites in the cavern were trying to find: the Nothing at the core of the coiled cosmos? I heard the words behind Joshua's words: God is everything; God is nothing. And I knew that he had received that illumination that had eluded the ascetics with their fasting and their self-mutilation, and the meditators in their niches, staring at eternity.

"Thank you for teaching me, Father," Joshua said.

"It was only my duty," said Joseph. "You will be a man soon; it will be time for me to take you to the Temple, so you can impress the priests with your knowledge of the Torah; it's almost time for you to be bar mitzvah."

"Father," said Joshua, "I will tell them all that I have received."

Only I noticed that, though they were speaking our mother tongue, Aramaic, Joshua had used a strange word from the old tongue for "that which I have received" — he had called it kabbalah.

When I finished my story, Paul took a long gulp of wine. I don't think it was what he expected. "You know the rest, I'm sure," I said. There is a garbled version of Joshua's bar mitzvah gone mad in those Greek biographies that circulate among the Christianoi. He did preach the wisdom he had received at the summit of the tree. He preached, and no one understood him. And they said, "So this is the kind of incoherent theology the Carpenter has been teaching his son." And after, I bore Joseph sons and daughters, and he became ever more estranged from my enigmatic firstborn; and he never did say aloud the words I heard so clearly in his mind, on a mountaintop in India: he never did say *I love you.*

And my son and I spoke even less. I had seen his vision in which he slew the mother-dragon; and I think he had seen mine, seen that we shared that which cannot be spoken of; even though it was in a dream, and in a country of dreams, there are truths too deep to be spoken except in dreams.

I wanted Paul to leave me alone; I was not done mourning. Crucifixion, you know, negates man's very humanity. There is no dignity in it, though perhaps, in future generations, when it is no longer practiced, men will come to see in it some mystic quality.

"So you see," I told Paul, "there's nothing here for you; mysterious hallucinations, vivid dreams, that's all there was. And when we returned to Nazareth, there was no more magic."

"Nonsense, Miriam," he said. "Everything you've told me is wonderful. Now I feel as if I'm waking up from a transcendent vision, trying to grasp the images before they fade away ... trying to hold on."

"I don't even know if it really happened," I said.

"It'll need editing, of course," Paul said. "But you can trust me to extract the truth out of this chaos of myth and symbol. I mean, forgive me, Miriam, but you are the vessel, not the drinker; you are the platter, not the fruit. There's no dragon left in you; your son has slain the past."

My husband had feared the she-demon in me, whom he sometimes called Ashtaroth, the goddess of lust; the Christianoi would defang this devil and take away even her womanhood; that was part of what Paul meant, I think, by "editing." He would extract from my son's life a shining arc of sin and redemption; as a woman should, God's mother would sit in a corner of his church, and speak only when spoken to.

Why not? If we are to believe the ascetics in the country beyond the edge of the world, the ultimate truth is a great nothing. Joshua told my husband that he had ascended to the top of the tree, and there had found nothing. Nothing meaning nothing, or nothing meaning that which is so beyond absolute that nothing can describe it?

Now I am an old woman in a small house in Ephesus, waiting for death. From time to time I visit the Great Mother in her Temple here, one of the world's seven wonders; she is a hundred cubits tall, and I am a little woman, and very frail now; but there are days when I do have the hubris to call her "sister".

Years ago, long after my interview with the man who called himself Paul, I arrived in Ephesus and bought this small house with money that my sons and daughters had collected for me from people I did not know. I planted a fruit tree in the center of the atrium. The tree stands tall now, amid the statues of vanquished gods. One day its ten branches will be mighty enough to support my tiny frame; one day its topmost branch will stretch all the way up to the end of the sky.

That day, I think, I'll climb that tree, climb all the way to God.

A Lap Dance with the Lobster Lady☙

"Love," said Ronnie's dad, "can be found in the darkest places. There is no corner of the universe so degraded, so vile, so irredeemable as to hinder the nurturing of love; love grows without water, without warmth, without light ... it is the ultimate fungus."

Ronnie Desmond was only five years old at the time, but then as now he always took his daddy's words to heart, because Mr. Desmond was wearing his special glasses. They were round and thick and they magnified his eyes, and he only put them on for work, or when he wanted to impart some particular pearl of wisdom to his son. Ronnie's dad knew everything about the dark places. He was an undertaker, the only one in Willowcreek.

Ronnie didn't spend much time looking for love as he grew older. After all, if love was everywhere, why even look? When the time came, when he needed it, it would surely pop right up and grab him and take him where he needed to go. Meanwhile, he would take things as they came.

It was a good thing Ronnie didn't feel the need to look for love, because all the way through kindergarten, elementary school, and junior high, Ronnie had no friends. It was not that he was socially inept, or ugly, or clumsy. He was turning into quite a handsome boy, with nice straight teeth, immaculately faded hair, a rare but winning smile; an average student, a soso athlete, in no sense a loner. He had many acquaintances. No one minded sitting next to him at lunch, or bringing him into the conversation.

But they all knew about his dad. Perhaps it was their imagination, but Ronnie had an aura about him. Or an odor. Something to do with death. And so these acquaintances of Ronnie's would only go so for to get close to him. They never wanted to spend the night. They never wanted him to stay over, either.

Even Ronnie's mother had never spent the night at their house. She had met and loved and married his dad when he was in the service, stationed in Schweinfurt. Dad came back to take over the business, with his new wife and baby in tow; and in the middle of the night she upped and left him, and took the bus to California. Everyone in town knew the story. Everyone in town knew everything. It was that kind of town.

It is not terribly surprising, then, that this angelic, deferential young man, who lived in a pictureperfect neighborhood, in a pretty ranchstyle house with a wellequipped basement, reached his senior high school year with a detailed theoretical knowledge, but no practical experience, of sex.

And as for love, he never thought of it at all.

That is, until he and Delbert Russo stole Delbert's cousin's '66 Impala and went to the carnival at Hangman's Holler....

To call it stealing would be an overstatement. People didn't steal things in Willowcreek. Doors were left unlocked. Delbert's cousin's '66 Impala had been sitting around for a year, ever since he'd been sent to the penitentiary. Not that he'd committed a crime. No one committed crimes in Willowcreek. Now Hangman's Holler was a different matter. Sodom and Gomorrah had nothing on the place, if you believed half of what Brother Thurston had to say every Sunday.

Delbert's cousin had been about halfway through restoring the car, and it had sat in the garage with the keys still in it.

"I'm sick of looking at that fucking car," Delbert said one day. "Let's go somewhere."

"Nowhere to go," said Ronnie.

"That's where you're wrong," said Delbert. "There's always somewhere to go."

"Yeah? Where?"

"There's Hangman's Holler."

"Been there," said Ronnie. "There's nothing there."

"You've been there in the daytime," said Delbert, "working with your dad, helping him load some stiff into the hearse. I heard it's a lot different at night."

"Could be." Ronnie had only been there twice. His dad once tried to expand his business by putting a 10% off coupon in the Hangman's Holler paper. But after a while he decided the extra business wasn't worth the onehour drive.

"I hear there's a carnival there this week."

"I've been to a carnival."

"I hear they got hookers there. I hear you're a virgin."

"Yeah."

"Me too."

"We must be the only ones at Willowcreek High," said Ronnie.

They were standing in front of the open garage. It was sunset. Ronnie didn't know Delbert that well; he was the only new kid in school that year. Delbert had moved in with his aunt and uncle about the time that his cousin had gone to the penitentiary. His parents were dead, and Delbert never mentioned them. They had sat next to each other in Mrs. Fortescue's English class all semester, barely exchanging a word. But every day for a week now, walking the two miles home from school, since neither of them owned a car, Delbert had struck up a conversation with Ronnie just as he was about to turn into the walkway to his house; today was the first time Ronnie had stayed all the way until sunset. He had never been invited inside. It all made him a little nervous. He wondered whether he had found his first friend.

"Why would me and you want to take off in a stolen car and have adventures in the middle of the night?" Ronnie said. "That's the kind of thing only best friends would do."

"Well," Delbert said, "truth is, I've been watching you."

"How come?"

Delbert smiled. "We got a lot in common," he said. "And one of these days ... I need to get into your basement."

"Why?" said Ronnie.

"I want to see a woman," said Delbert. "I mean, really see one."

Well, because it was Friday night, and because there was nothing scheduled at the funeral home for the weekend, and because his dad had gone to a headstone manufacturer's convention in Philadelphia, and because Delbert hadn't flinched when Ronnie hinted that this kind of escapade might turn the two outcasts into best friends, and because it was the path of least resistance, Ronnie got into the passenger seat of the half-restored '66 Impala as Delbert turned the key, made the car lurch into drive, and the drove up to the last and only stop sign in Willowcreek, where the railroad tracks marked the county line.

Night fell the moment they crossed those tracks — it was that time of year. The road to Hangman's Holler wound tightly around the foothills. The woods came right up to the shoulder of Route 267. For the first fifteen minutes or so, Ronnie was nervous; he kept thinking they'd be pulled over, if not for stealing the vehicle, then for speeding or reckless driving, because quiet, mousy, undernourished-looking Delbert drove like a madman. But after a while Ronnie got used to the weird feeling in his stomach, and started to get into the adventure of it. It was strange to be actually going somewhere on a Friday night with a friend. Usually, Ronnie spent Friday night helping out his father in the basement, or watching the Spice Channel into the wee hours. That was where he got his theoretical knowledge about sex. Could this be the night he finally tried the real thing?

If Ronnie was finally making friends, he wondered if love could be far behind. Ronnie read a lot of books, so he knew that people's lives move through a series of pivotal plot points, of epiphanies ... perhaps tonight would be one of them.

They didn't talk much as the woods reeled by. There was hardly anyone else on the road. There was a full moon. The sky was luminous; bright silver clung to the trees. Oldies blared on the radio.

"So," Delbert said after a while, "you looking to get laid tonight?"

"I don't know," said Ronnie.

"You a funny bunny?"

"No," said Ronnie, though he wasn't sure what Delbert meant. "What about you? Maybe we'll both get some."

"You think about it much?" Delbert said. "Fucking, I mean."

"I guess."

"Watched a lotta pornos?"

"Maybe."

"They move too much," said Delbert. "The bitches, they move too much. Can't pin 'em down."

At the top of the hill, the road plunged steeply toward Hangman's Holler. It was there that, as they coasted round a corner much too fast, the Impala overheated and Delbert braked sharply and pulled into an overlook.

"Shit!" he said. Ronnie liked it when his friend cussed. It sounded cool.

Delbert popped the hood. Acrid smoke poured into the night. Ronnie stepped out. The night air was chill. The smoke glowed in the moonlight. The woods stretched in every direction. It was like a horror movie.

"I guess this blows our adventure," Ronnie said ruefully.

"Bullshit," said Delbert. He poked around under the hood and finally pulled out a hose. "Just gotta replace this." He threw Ronnie the keys and told him to unlock the trunk.

The trunk of Delbert's cousin's Impala was pretty amazing. Ronnie counted about six rifles and a whole lot of knives a Bowie knife, an Xacto knife, straight razors, a rusted butcher knife. Delbert rooted through the stuff and selected a hunting rifle and a knife. "Wait here," he said, and strode into the woods.

It was getting cold, so Ronnie waited in the car. It seemed like a lot of time was passing, and Ronnie was pretty sure he wasn't going to get to the carnival that night. Then he heard the rifle go bang. He sat there waiting to see what Delbert would come up with.

Delbert finally showed up. He held up what looked like a piece of hose. Ronnie got out to help him. "Put this shit back for me," Delbert said, tossing him the knife and the rifle. Ronnie threw them in the trunk. The knife handle was slick and oozy. Ronnie knew what blood felt like; there was always plenty to mop up in the basement.

He joined Delbert, who was tinkering under the hood. "You can't watch," Delbert said. "Go and start the car for me."

Delbert did something with his hands. The raised hood prevented Ronnie from seeing exactly what. But there was some kind of whirling mist ... a flash of cold blue light. Like what you'd see in a magic show. Ronnie turned the key in the ignition. It started up fine, and in a few moments they were heading downhill, toward Hangman's Holler.

Ronnie didn't want to pry, but curiosity got the better of him.

'How'd you find a hose in the woods?"

“Got it off a deer,” said Delbert. “The big intestine just about the same width.”

“Yeah, but ... it’s flesh ... not rubber. I mean ... how did you get it to...”

“I’m good at fixing stuff,” Delbert said. “I can assemble anything ... it runs in the family. Well, except for my cousin. He takes shit apart all right, but he can never put it back together again.”

“So why’s he in the penitentiary?”

“Just told you, didn’t I? I wish you’d listen.”

And Delbert wouldn’t talk again until they pulled into the parking lot of the carnival.

Before they even got to the gate, they ran into two girls from Willowcreek. They were smoking by the ticket booth. Ronnie knew one of them: she was Missy Cooper, from Mrs. Fortescue’s English class, a perky blonde who always had her nose in the air. She’d never said a word to Ronnie before, but she seemed a lot different. She had a lot of makeup on. The moonlight made her lipstick look deep purple, almost black. The dress she had on was a size or two too small.

“Well, well,” she said, “the couple most likely to succeed ... the retard and the ghoul finally paired off, I see.”

Ronnie thought Delbert would get mad, but he just laughed. Missy offered them cigarettes. Delbert took one.

“Whatcha doing away from your daddy’s basement?” said Missy. “Your hormones finally kicked in?”

“He’s just looking for love,” Delbert said. “Same as you.”

She laughed and puffed and spluttered.

“I never saw you smoke before,” said Ronnie. “And you never spoke to me in school.”

“We ain’t in Willowcreek now,” she said. “We checked our morals at the railroad tracks. You know Amanda?”

Neither of them did. Missy’s friend was one of those dumpylooking ones that attractive girls always seem to have as a best friend. The two of them made Ronnie uncomfortable somehow, although Delbert started chatting with both of them.

Eventually Ronnie said, “We should go in, Delbert. Or we’ll miss everything.”

“You got everything you need right here,” Missy said, blowing a smoke ring in his face.

But Ronnie could see the lights, and smell the hot dogs and stale beer, and he forked over his two dollars and went inside, with Delbert following behind.

Ronnie had been to carnivals before ... some of these same rides had been in Willowcreek last year ... but there was something different about this one. It wasn't just because they were in a different town. The people were different. Maybe because it was late there weren't that many kids. Their faces were pale, their cheeks hollow, their cotton candy flaccid and trailing in filaments in the wind. There was a lot of mud. The ferris wheel, dominating the field, was missing many of its lights, and it stayed stationary, waiting for a new customer. Two teens made out in the uppermost seats. A dwarf barker touted a freak show; a microcephalic giant announced a haunted train ride. The wind whipped leaves and candy wrappers into little hurricanes. A brass band wheezed out a tired waltz. Most people seemed to be moving in one particular direction, toward a tent at the far end of the carnival, past an alley lined with shooting, tossing, horseracing games. A man in a tuxedo and cloak stood at the entrance, disgorging bats from a top hat.

"It's some kind of a magic show," Ronnie said. "Let's go."

"Those people don't know what they're doing," said Delbert. "Bunch of fakes."

"It seems like the only happening place around here. C'mon."

As they neared the tent, Ronnie saw that the crowd was more frantic, more animated ... the hot dogs smelled more fresh ... the colors of people's clothes were brighter ... the keen air more bracing ... the music bouncier. Something's about to happen, he thought. And, right at the entrance, as they were paying to get inside, something did. Ronnie Desmond fell in love.

It was a face. A flash of crimson dress. A startling swirl of fieryred hair. And eyes that were as green as a handful of freshpulled grass. Eyes that were turned on him, that seemed to be looking at him alone ... and lips just parting, on the verge of speaking ... of saying something only he could hear. And then there was a whiff of ... some alien perfume ... the air from another planet. It was the momentary scent that convinced Ronnie this was love.

Ronnie had never fallen in love before, but he knew what it was right away. He had read enough descriptions, and seen enough movies, to get the general idea. The fluttering in the pit of his stomach, for one. And the brightness of the image. Everything around that face seemed to have all its color drained away ... their faces seemed as lifeless as the corpses in his basement. And Ronnie knew that this is how love comes, like Newton's apple, like an anvil from the sky.

The face was there for only moments. Then there was nothing but the sea of dead faces, and Delbert was pushing him into the tent. Who was that woman? How could he see her again? What had she been about to say to him?

The magic show was already in progress. They managed to make it all the way to the front. The benches were hard, like church pews. There was dust and straw and smoke. A hawker came up the aisle with a tray of soggy hot dogs. Ronnie wanted to get up and look for the woman, but people were squeezed in so tight that he couldn't leave.

The magician's name was Dazzo the Dazzling. He had a cape and a tux and a wand, and he hurled himself across the stage with a breathless energy, but there was a sadness about him, and his pretty assistant never smiled. She was just going through the routine, dancing, curtsying, waving her arms. The show was nothing special. Rabbits pulled out of hats, coins popping out of children's ears.

"This is boring," Delbert whispered. 'Let's get out of here."

"I heard that!" cried Dazzo the Dazzling. He wagged a finger in Delbert's face, and Delbert, oddly chastened, sort of hunched down further into the bench. "This weasel thinks I'm just some secondrate illusionist," he announced,with a sweeping gesture to the audience. "But all of you know better, don't you? What are we all waiting for?" he cried. "What grand deception's yet to come?"

The audience was silent. Until a lone voice, a little kid's voice, piped up: "The Lobster Lady."

"Well done, young man!" said the magician, and his assistant, in her tattered showgirl outfit, did a little twirl of the arms. "Well ... since I see I am boring our guest ... with my tawdry little warmup act ... shall we cut to the chase?"

Scattered applause now. Ronnie perked up a little. Because, all of sudden, he had caught that scent again. He knew that the woman was nearby. There was an exotic fragrance ... perhaps some tropical flower ... mingled with something far more familiar ... the perfume of decay, which sometimes wafted up into Ronnie's bedroom through cracks in the floorboards.

"Cutting," said Dazzo the Dazzling, "is the word of the evening. You have all seen women sawn in half ... but tonight you will see more than a woman and more than a saw."

Dazzo's assistant banged portentously on a gong. A drape was whisked up into the roof of the tent, and behind it, on a wheelchair, sat the woman. The stench of putrid flowers drenched his nostrils. The assistant wheeled the woman toward the front of the makeshift stage. "May I introduce," said the magician, "the tragic figure of Veronica ... the Lobster Lady!"

The Lobster Lady smiled. Right at Ronnie. He stared at her. She stared back. It happened again ... the color draining away from everything but her eyes, her hair, the crimson of her dress.

"The torso of a beautiful woman ... the mangled and deformed lower body of a monster," said Dazzo. "In due course, you shall see the true horror of this lady's condition."

Workmen were carrying in two coffinlike boxes, and a burly helper lifted the Lobster Lady ... so very gingerly ... and placed her in one of the boxes. It was the standard box that women are sawn in half in; every magician has one. The workmen stood the boxes up, side by side. Each one was inscribed with mystic signs, hieroglyphs, suns and moons.

"Boring," said Delbert under his breath. "I know how this works. She tucks her legs behind, you know. There's a secret space for them."

"I heard that!" said Dazzo, leaning over the platform and practically shouting in Delbert's face. "This is not Carpentry 101, young man. This is the bending of the wall between illusion and reality. You of all people should know what I mean."

Ronnie saw them gaze into each other's eyes. He remembered the blue flash of light and the Impala that now had a piece of a onceliving creature inside it. But he didn't think about that for long. He was still looking at Veronica, the Lobster Lady. A little doorway in the coffin revealed her face. A second doorway, where her legs would be, was closed.

Dazzo leaped back up onto the stage. "I will now require the assistance of a lady from the audience," he said.

A murmur of "Me, me, me" around the tent. Behind the murmur, the rustle of the wind outside.

"I'll do it," said a familiar voice. Ronnie turned to see Missy Cooper striding up the aisle with her fat friend in tow.

"Yeah," said Amanda. "She'll do it." Stars in the fat girl's eyes; a leer on the cheerleader's lips.

"We have an outoftowner," said Dazzo, grinning.

"Yeah. I'm from the other side of the hill."

As they helped Missy into the other box, Dazzo began to relate the Lobster Lady's sad little tale. "Deformed, as I said, deformed. But the Lobster Lady yearns to walk like other ladies. She yearns, perchance, to pirouette, to prance, to skip, to skate. But how, with the abominations she calls legs? It's time for a little creative surgery."

And as a honkytonk piano struck up a discordant tango Dazzo started to saw with a vengeance. First one, then the other. And both women were gazing out at the audience from their little doorways.

"It's fake," said Delbert. "If it was real, the bitch'd be screaming."

"Shut up," said Amanda, who had squeezed onto the bench next to Delbert. "You're ruining the atmosphere."

Presently, as the music crescendoed, Dazzo the Dazzling finished sawing through both boxes. He clapped his hands, and workmen lifted up the two top halves and solemnly swapped them.

Dazzo closed the door on Missy's face.

The music died down to a whisper. The pianist was just vamping now, playing the same chords over and over as the magician began to intone.

Are you ready, my dear?" he said. "Are you ready to dance? In the harsh world outside this tent, you're a miserable cripple who must be wheeled from place to place ... but here ... inside the confines of this magical sarcophagus ... you can know what it's like to be as ordinary mortals...."

He flung open the bottom door. "Behold!" he cried. he folded the doors back and now there was an unobstructed view save for a narrow strip of wood of one whole woman a woman with the upper body of an angel and the legs of Missy Cooper.

"Time for a pirouette, my dear," said Dazzo the Dazzling.

He took the Lobster Lady by the hand and snapped the fingers of his free hand. Spun her around inside that box. The torso spun ... the eyes fixed on Ronnie, the head not turning till the last possible moment ... the torso spun, the legs spun, they were like a single being.

"Who will you dance with, Veronica, my dear?" said Dazzo. "Who in this crowd of admirers do you fancy? Who will adore you tonight? To whom will you bequeath your undying love?"

The throng fell silent. The Lobster Lady spoke, and her voice, to Ronnie, had a music of heartbreak and joy. "Tonight," said the

Lobster Lady, "I'll dance with the Messenger of Death ... the angel of Willowcreek, who tends to the dead."

And she pointed a finger straight at Ronnie, who was already half out of his seat. He almost stumbled in his haste to reach her. Her hands were hot to the touch. The piano went into a slow waltz.

"Dance with me," she said.

She put a hand no his shoulder and another around his waist. He hardly knew what was happening because he couldn't stop looking into her eyes. The music tugged at him. He wanted to drag her out of the box and waltz with her across the hollow planks, but she could not leave her box, not without being ripped in two. So he held her, rocked her, and ... at long last ... felt her lips graze his.

"Soon this will be over," she said.

"No," he said. "I can't let it end. I love you."

"I know," she said. "But will you even love the way I really am?"

"Yes," he whispered, "yes, yes, yes."

No one in the audience heard them. They saw only a boy and a woman, waltzing in place, rocking each other slowly, back and forth, awkwardly, not quite in time to the music.

"In a few more seconds," she said, "you'll have to make a choice. You can go home tonight and never see me again, or you can take a step into my world ... and let me take a step into yours.."

"I'd do anything," Ronnie said.

"I know," said the Lobster Lady.

"How do you know?" he asked her. "How did you know I would be the one to fall in love with you tonight?"

"That was simple," said the Lobster Lady. "I've been watching you." And then she kissed him chastely, of course right in front of all those people, and told him where he could find her after the show.

The waltz came to an abrupt halt, and now there was a drumroll.

"Time," cried the magician, "for you to return those borrowed limbs ... for you to rejoin your horrifying body!" He waved Ronnie back to his seat. "But before we swap you back ... I want to show ..." he opened the face door of the other coffin "... just how horrifying your existence really is. Behold!" And he snapped open the lower portion of the casket. "Behold the tormented mutation that is the Lobster Lady!"

Missy Cooper looked down at where her own legs should be. There was only the long red dress ... and then ... forcing its way out from the sheer fabric ... she saw them. The audience saw them. Gasped. Screamed. The mass of pincers, claws, and tentacles writhed, snapped at the empty air, oozing a viscous rheum that smoked and sizzled as it dripped onto the floorboards.

The audience was shrieking and howling. There was applause. And on the face of Veronica, the Lobster Lady, Ronnie could see a profound sadness, a yearning, and ... mostly strangely, perhaps ... a certain compassion for her tormentors. In that moment, he knew that his love for her was real, and absolute as death.

Ronnie turned to Delbert. He wanted to communicate his feelings, his excitement, to this curious person who had suddenly become his best friend. But Delbert wasn't there. There was only Amanda, clapping furiously and hooting. And in moments the women had been swapped back, and the curtain had fallen to allow the Lobster Lady to be wheeled away ... the Dazzo the Dazzling was back to doing hackneyed card tricks downstage while the pianist vamped relentlessly.

He didn't look for Delbert too hard after he left the tent. Delbert could take care of himself. Instead, Ronnie went back out through the parking lot, to the row of trailers parked behind the grocery store, to the very last trailer, with a lone candle burning in window.

He knocked three times and opened the door. And there she was. Still in the scarlet dress. And his heart was still pounding, and his stomach was still fluttering, so he knew he was still in love.

"Come closer," she said. "You know I can't come to you, not easily."

He sat down in a battered armchair. There wasn't much else in the trailer, really. Nowhere to lie down, for example. Maybe the Lobster Lady slept in her wheelchair. He held both her hands in his and heard the rustling, clacking sound from beneath her skirts, and he knew what was making those noises, but he wasn't afraid. Why would he be? He had slept near corpses all his life. She gripped his hands tight. She pulled him to her, forehead to forehead, eyes to eyes, lips almost to lips; her breath was what contained that fetor of life and death.

"You want me," she said.

He nodded.

"How do you want me?"

"Um ... what am I supposed to say? Sex stuff, I guess," said Ronnie. "I think I'm supposed to want that."

"You know much about sex?" she said. "I'm thinking virgin."

"Is it that obvious?"

"Virgins have a distinctive odor. Their blood is sweet and pure. After a while, the blood gets corrupted; the life force gutters, spends itself. And the taste is gone."

"You talk like a vampire."

"Well, that's not too far from the truth," she said, "but you're not here for me to drain your blood. I just want you to know I'm older than you think."

"You mean like, thirty?"

A silvery laugh in the close, cramped air. "Thirty, thirty thousand, what difference does it make? You reach a certain plateau of pain ... it gets to be all the same."

"What do you want me to do now?"

"Come closer. Kiss me."

And he did. It was not so chaste this time. Her tongue tasted of cinnamon and decay. She reached around his shoulders, gripped them, ripped at his shirt so that he felt her nails rend the skin a little. "I want to tear the cloth," she whispered, "want to feel your flesh, want the tingle of your blood as it races to your heart ." He touched her breasts through the bloodred fabric, felt the nipples in the palms of his hands, jabbing like fleshy nails. Deftly her hands were unbuckling his belt. Beneath her skirts, unthinkable things pulsed and seethed. His pants slid to the floor and she embraced his buttocks, grinding his penis against her face. He was trembling. He held on tight. Her lips and tongue darted, flecked, teased, tickled, finally engulfed. He tried to hold on to the wheelchair's arms to steady himself, but she clutched him so tight that he staggered backward onto the plastic coated walls, and now she was on the floor, a legless woman slithering towards him on crustacean claws, her mouth straining at the height of his crotch. She screamed out her frustration; confused, he ejaculated. His thoughts were as wild as the wind that whipped up the gravel and debris and pelted the windows of the trailer. There was arousal, there was love, there was shame.

"It will never work!" she cried out. "Look at you ... slender, goldenhaired, young, unsullied ... you want me the way a boy should want a woman ... you want to plunge your manhood into a place that I don't have for you. This isn't love ... it's not even sex ... it's some grotesque simulacrum of love ... and I will always be a monster ... always, always, always, except for a few minutes each night ... when I feel the motion in another's legs ... the fire in another's groin ... and all done with smoke and mirrors ... all illusion, all emptiness. I don't even have the option of dying."

And as Ronnie lifted the Lobster Lady in his arms and tenderly put her back in her wheelchair, she began to weep. With every tear, the odor of sweetness and death intensified, and with every breath of her perfume, his love grew stronger, fueled as much by her pain as by his ecstasy. Her tears mingled with the semen on her cheeks. When he kissed them away, he tasted himself as well as her. Later, as she smoked a cigarette, he danced for her in the candlelight, letting her eyes play with his perfect young body, letting her make love to him in her mind, where she was a whole woman, able to fulfill and be fulfilled.

As he was getting dressed again, they talked.

"This can never happen again," the Lobster Lady said.

"Why not?" he protested.

"I can't do this to you. I know you're telling yourself, half a woman is better than none, but you're cheating yourself. You shouldn't love me if you can't make love to me."

"No," said Ronnie. "This can't end. I'm gonna make things right for you."

"And how will you do that?" the Lobster Lady said bitterly. "Will you get me a new lower torso?"

"I can do that," Ronnie said. "My dad gets them in all the time."

"And you know someone who can do real magic, not just give me the illusion of a real body for a few moments, inside the confines of a stage coffin? I don't think so."

"I have a friend," said Ronnie, "who can fix things real good."

He stood in the doorway of the trailer. It was getting on towards dawn. He noticed that the wind had finally subsided. One by one the lights on the ferris wheel were winking out.

She stared at him intently, as though, he thought, to engrave his features on her memory, which was a strange thing, since he meant to see her again, and soon. Then she said, "I knew, Ronnie Desmond, that you would be the one to help me."

"I never told you my last name," he said. "You read my mind or something?"

"I work in a sideshow," she said. "We're all clairvoyants around here." Then, giggling, she flashed the student I.D. she had fished out of his pants pocket during the throes of their unfinished lovemaking.

She tossed, he caught.

A strange thought crossed his mind: Was I set up?

Delbert was waiting for him at the gate. He was already in his car. As they pulled out of the lot, Ronnie saw four cop cars blocking the road toward Willowcreek; they made the shape of a cross, and at the center he could see the fat girl, Amanda, who was waving her hands and hollering and shrieking. They were carrying someone away on a stretcher.

"Fancy that," said Delbert.

"Do you think it's Missy Cooper? Is she hurt?"

"That would explain why Amanda's so bent out of shape. Every fat girl needs a cheerleader to lean on."

"Should we stop?"

"Nah," Delbert said. "Gotta go home."

They arrived in Willowcreek at dawn, and Ronnie thought he'd sleep in, but whenever he closed his eyes, he saw things. Deep sea creatures. Monsters of the ocean. Stuff from bad scifi movies. It was stupid, but he couldn't sleep until he drained half a bottle of Nyquil.

When he woke up, his dad had come home from the convention, and he was already in the basement working on Missy Cooper.

She was lying on one of Mr. Desmond's work tables, having the fluids sucked out of her. She was in pretty bad shape.

"That's Missy Cooper," said Ronnie. "She goes to my school ... I saw her ... last night ... alive."

"You were in Hangman's Holler?" said Ronnie's dad, peering at him through his glasses ... those glasses.

Ronnie was nervous. He had never been that far from home without telling his dad before. He stood there, looking pretty guilty, he was sure, but all his dad said was, "Now you make sure, next time you go on a jaunt like that, that you take a couple of these with you." He rooted around in a drawer on the table that Missy's corpse was lying on, and pulled out a couple of rubbers. "This is where they're kept. I don't want to hear any more about it. Be a good boy, now, and help me empty all this blood."

"How did she die?" said Ronnie, as he hastened to replace the bucket of body fluids and to pour the full one down the sink.

His dad turned up the suction and asked for his makeup kit. "You know that's none of our business, Ronnie," said Mr. Desmond. "But they're calling it an accident, and I don't want you to say otherwise; Willowcreek's a good town, a safe town, and we don't want word getting out about any of this sort of thing."

Missy was covered with bruises and lacerations. There were stab wounds, too. There was an open gash between her breasts; her sternum had been cracked, like maybe with a hammer, and she had no heart.

"It doesn't look like an accident to me," Ronnie said. "Don't they want to keep the body, do tests, forensics, stuff like that?"

"The family wants a quick, quiet, closedcoffin funeral," said his dad. "We don't the press here. You know what a madhouse that can be. You saw those schoolhouse shootings on TV. I think the Coopers are doing the right thing. It's not like they can bring their daughter back. They're good Christian people, and they know about forgiveness."

"But don't they want to know who did it?"

"God knows, son," said Mr. Desmond, "and that's good enough for the folks in Willowcreek."

"Closed coffin?" said Ronnie, who was getting the germ of an idea in his head. "When's the funeral?"

"Tomorrow," said his dad. "Hold her head up for me. She needs to look real pretty for the viewing."

And that was when it all fell into place for Ronnie. He had the germ of a plan, if only all the pieces would fit together.

He went on helping his father, but he was distracted. Usually he enjoyed being with his dad, bonding with him working with the corpses was really the only time he felt they were a family but today he was impatient. It took an extra long time to stitch Missy up so that she'd hold together without leaking. Whoever did this to her had been real thorough. He wondered if it was a sex crime. He'd seen those on TV.

The job went on until way past dinnertime, but his dad didn't take a break. They ordered Chinese and worked on Missy's face over duck chow mein. The face and hands were all they'd see at the viewing, so they had to be good. "It's a good thing they didn't decide to bury her in her cheerleading uniform," said Mr. Desmond. "We'd have had to pull an all-nighter on the legs."

Ronnie knew that when the makeup was all done he would be able to leave. His dad always liked to spend some time alone with a job when it was all done. Fussing with it, admiring his own handiwork, especially if the client was a nicelooking young woman. You couldn't blame him. By the time his dad was done, Missy Cooper could've won Miss Dead America.

As soon as he could, Ronnie raced over to Delbert's house. He found him by the garage, tinkering with the guts of the '66 Impala. It was sunset again, but there was enough light porch to see past Delbert's shoulders and catch a glimpse of the engine. It was just as Ronnie suspected; the inside of that Impala wasn't all metal and rubber and plastic. Some of the hoses, for instance, had to be organic, from the way they gleamed and dripped blood. Under the purr of the engine Ronnie could hear the beating of a heart.

"Hi, Ronnie," Delbert said, not looking around.

"Something wrong with the car again?"

"Nah," said Delbert. "Just, you know, tinkering. Bit here, bit there. One day my cousin will come home, and then this thing'll never get fixed right; told you he's no good at that."

"Ronnie, can we go to Hangman's Holler again tonight?"

"You got laid, didn't you!" He slammed the hood down, got a beer from a fridge in the garage, tossed it to Ronnie. "Here. Celebrate."

Ronnie caught it, didn't open it, went on, "This woman ... I met her there ... man ... I think I love her. And she's not right. Needs fixing. I told her, I got a friend who can put anything together, doesn't need a Chilton's, and well, I kinda sorta volunteered your help."

Delbert laughed. "You people always think with your dicks."

"What do you mean, we people? You're like me, and you know it."

"Not just like you," said Delbert, "or you wouldn't be needing my help."

Ronnie couldn't argue. He just waited until Delbert had paced back and forth for a while, thinking it over he guessed. Finally he stopped. "You in love with her?" he asked Ronnie.

"Of course I'm in love," Ronnie said. "I'm ripping apart everything I've ever known for her. It's got to be love. I feel bigger than myself with her. I feel I could conquer the universe."

"She gave you head, huh," said Delbert. "You fool. Veronica's blowjobs are famous in four counties."

"She's hurting, Delbert! I can save her!"

Delbert said, "Then maybe I should explain something. What I do ... it ain't scientific. There's no guarantee of it. I can put stuff back together perfect, sometimes, but that don't mean it can get back up and walk to the bus."

"So it was you," said Ronnie.

"What? Oh, you mean—"

"Missy Cooper. It was you. You're some kind of sex killer."

"Not really, Ronnie. That's my cousin. I'm way too well brought up to do anything like that. I'll kiss a girl, but I sure as hell won't violate her, even if she's dead."

"Then why—"

"It's my carburetor," said Delbert. "I never have enough spare parts."

"But she was all tore up!"

"Told you," Delbert said. "I was just taking a look inside. That's why you're gonna show me your dad's basement one day. So I can get a better look. Figure out how they're put together. I put everything back ... except the engine, of course, I needed that. But the seams don't show. Well, hardly."

"It's going to be different with the Lobster Lady," said Ronnie. "She'll get up again. She can't die."

And so they went back to Hangman's Holler, to fetch the Lobster Lady, to make her whole again.

When they reached Hangman's Holler, the carnival was over. Only the ferris wheel remained ... and a few of the trailers ... and a lone gypsy fortune teller squatting by the road. But the trailer of the Lobster Lady still glowed with candlelight. Telling Delbert to wait in the corner, Ronnie went and rapped on the door.

Then he went in.

She was just as he had left her. It was as if no time had passed at all. They were in each other's arms, and he was telling her it would be all right, rocking her, cradling her like a lost child.

"We'll get you your new legs," he said. "The same legs you tried on last night, the legs you danced with me on, those slender lithe cheerleader legs ... oh, Veronica, tomorrow we'll dance for real...."

"And you'll fuck me for real, won't you?"

"Oh, yes," he said. "Yes, yes. I'll be inside you forever."

She kissed him, long and lovingly, and then told him, "Only an act of ultimate love and sacrifice can set me free."

"Is it a curse?" asked Ronnie. Curses were so romantic.

"In a way," said the Lobster Lady. And Ronnie felt like a hero in an ancient saga; he was mighty, he was full of magic, he could redeem lost souls.

Because the Desmonds' ranch house was also a funeral home, the front door led to a big anteroom with a nondenominational chapel to one side so that the customers could bring in a minister of their choice. There was a big chest just outside the chapel door that had all every religion separate, in a cardboard box: a Catholic box, a Baptist box, a Lutheran box, even a Jewish box, though they hadn't used that since the last Jews moved away from Willowcreek three years ago.

Usually, the night before a viewing, Mr. Desmond would pick out the appropriate CD and let it run on autorepeat, so that the right vibes would be set up for the ceremony. The Coopers had selected a Tammy Wynette medley, played on a Wurlitzer organ by Willowcreek's own Miss Tanya Fisher. The selfproduced CD was a countywide bestseller. "Stand By Your Man" had been Missy's favorite song, though in life she had never managed to stand by one for more than a couple of weeks. Miss Fisher's sprightly interpretation rang down the aisles of the empty chapel and poured into the anteroom from speakers hidden behind two plastic Chinese vases.

Ronnie wheeled the Lobster Lady into the anteroom and Delbert followed. Ronnie was about to snap on a light, but the Lobster Lady stopped him. "I don't like it," she said, "when it's too bright." Even so, there was plenty of moonlight; there was a skylight in the antechamber. But Missy wasn't on display yet.

"She's probably still in the basement," Ronnie said.

"Good," said Delbert. "I'd rather work in the basement. I don't like it here."

Ronnie led his friends around to the back of the house, where there was a wide doorway with a special ramp for hauling equipment, because the wheelchair wouldn't be able to make it down the regular stairs next to the kitchen refrigerator.

The only way to work in the basement was under overhead fluorescent light, and the Lobster Lady didn't like that very much; she sat in the shadow of a filing cabinet, shading her eyes with her sleeve.

Missy lay on the table. She was all ready to be put in the coffin, which was the latest model, the Jackie O., from that supply house in Philadelphia where the coffins are all named after celebrities. The coffin lay on the floor, ready for the transfer; it was all white and shiny, with a pretty pink inlay and a big red heart in glaze enamel on the lid, lined with pink satin. Missy's dress was on a hanger next to the embalming fluid vats. Missy herself ... well, Mr. Desmond's work was legendary in Willowcreek. Even though his dad had said he was only going to do a quick patchwork job on the legs, he had actually matched their tint exactly to the hands and face, and he'd picked just the right blush, just the right delicate shade of lipstick.

"Who'd have thought the slut of Willowcreek High could look so innocent," Delbert said. He stepped up to the table.

"What's next? You saw her in half?" said the Lobster Lady.

"Hell no, ma'am," said Delbert. "This bitch is a jigsaw puzzle. I put her together so well you couldn't slide a dollar bill between the cracks ... but I still know where the joins are. Even through Mr. Desmond's perfect paint job."

Delbert ran his hands over Missy's dead body. Like a really good auto mechanic's, his touch held a kind of tenderness; he loved his work. He caressed her inert breasts, and Ronnie could tell that the hands remembered past acquaintance, relived a dayold passion; Delbert closed his eyes, breathed deeply the perfume of embalming.

His hands went lower now, down the blonde mound, applying gentle pressure, seeking out something. His eyes opened for a moment, glared; he yanked out a used rubber and threw it on the floor. "Ew," he said, "someone didn't clean up after themselves." So that was why his dad kept the condoms in that drawer, Ronnie thought, as he bent down and carefully flicked it into the trash. Veronica watched now and then, but mostly she had her sleeve over her eyes; Ronnie squeezed her other hand. She must be afraid, he thought. Anyone would be. But she was going to be reborn. There would be new life out of the dust of death. He was healing her. He was only doing what Jesus did, what the apostles did. And maybe Delbert was a sex killer, but it would have been unChristian not to forgive him.

Delbert found what he was looking for. Like a ninjitsu master, he raised one hand in a chopping gesture, channeled all his inner strength into that hand ... in fact, Ronnie could have sworn that the lower edge of the palm glowed with a fierce blue light ... and drew it across Missy's hips like a giant scalpel. Missy cracked in two. Quickly, cleanly ... just as Delbert said it would ... like two sections of a jigsaw puzzle.

"One bottom half coming up," said Delbert, giggling a little. "I was afraid it wouldn't cleave right."

The Lobster Lady's grip tightened. Delbert hefted the top half of Missy into the coffin, and turned to Ronnie and Veronica. "Now," he said, "you're absolutely sure she can't die?"

Ronnie was sweating. Veronica had told him that more than once, but then no one had sliced her in half before ... well, not really. Or had they?

"I can't," said the Lobster Lady. "I'm one of those archetype things. I go on and on and on."

"Even so," said Delbert, "I want you to be sure you want to do it. You've never been taken apart before. A rock, you know, has fault lines; a car has screws and bolts; on a woman, you have to make the places where they break."

"How do you know I don't have fault lines?" said Veronica. "I've been sawn in half a million times. You don't think I'm used to it by now?"

"But that," said Delbert, "was just makebelieve."

"So is the universe," said the Lobster Lady.

And so Ronnie helped Delbert wheel a second table next to the first. With the utmost tenderness, he lifted the Lobster Lady, taking care that her lower half pointed away from him, laying her down on the metal, cushioning her head with one of his dad's cosmetic boxes. He helped her unbutton her dress. It pulled away easily, and he saw all of his beloved for the first time. No face was more beautiful than hers. No skin was more delicate. No breasts were firmer or more smoothly rounded. Just beneath her navel the nightmare began: the claws, the tentacles, the slimy exoskeleton. Dark veins pulsed beneath the slick gray scales. A fishy, pussy rheum oozed, glistened, dripped slowly onto the floor, smoking when it hit the unclad concrete. Acid, thought Ronnie, acid on concrete always makes that hissing noise. Gently, very gently, he kissed her brow, her eyelids, her closed lips. She was trembling. He knew she was afraid, in spite of her belief that she would live forever.

Seeing her helpless like this, even knowing that her upper body segued into a crustacean monstrosity, he felt all the symptoms of love again: the fluttering in his loins, the lightheadedness, the hardness in his loins. He wished Delbert weren't there. He wanted so much to, to

No. Delbert pulled him away. "This part," he said, "you can't stay for. Trade secrets, you know. Classified information."

"But you let me watch up to now," Ronnie protested.

"Now comes the moment of truth. The holy of holies. There's always one secret chamber of the heart that no one else can enter. You know all that. You've read books. The actual moment of change is always a hidden moment." And Delbert, without changing from his dirty jeans, actually looked and sounded different ... like a priest, almost.

"She needs me to be with her," said Ronnie, gazing at her beseeching eyes.

"No," said Delbert. "You go and open the trunk of my car, and bring me my toolbox. And the skillsaw, and the long skinny knife with the blue handle. You can leave them at the top of the stairs. Then, you just go into the chapel and wait," said Delbert Russo. "And go over the cover story in your mind. Over and over. You can't afford any errors."

"It's all right, my darling," said the Lobster Lady softly. "I'll be brave."

"I love you," said Ronnie Desmond, and tiptoed from the room.

At five in the morning, Ronnie's dad didn't wake up. Ronnie had turned off the alarm.

At fivethirty, Missy was laying in her coffin, in the viewing area of the anteroom. The top side of the lid was open; her family and friends would see and touch her only from the shoulders up. When the minister arrived for the service, they would close the lid completely, and no one would ever see Missy Cooper's face again.

At six, Ronnie, slumped over and snoring in the front pew of the chapel, snapped awake. He hurried to the kitchen, knocked on the door to the basement.

"I'm cleaning up," Delbert said. The door was locked. "You can't come in yet. Just follow the plan. Everything's gonna be fine."

"Can't I see her?"

"No," Delbert said. "You'll see her when you see her."

At eight o'clock, Ronnie brought his dad breakfast in bed, nudged him gently to wake him.

"Shit," his dad murmured, "they'll be here in a couple hours, and I haven't even put the girl in her casket yet."

"It's okay, dad. I ... I didn't want to wake you ... you really needed your rest ... that convention in Philadelphia, this rush job ... you know. I made you an omelette. And I took care of the whole thing. It's all set up."

"Really? You sure?"

"Heck, Dad," said Ronnie, "I watched you often enough."

His dad sat up in the bed. Ham omelettes were his favorite breakfast, and Ronnie had toasted a cinnamon bagel too. "You know, son," said Mr. Desmond, "there comes a time in a man's life when he sees his son coming into his own ... and he's gotta be ready to let go ... to hand on the burdens ... welcome to the company ...

partner." And his dad kissed him on the cheek and patted him on the back and showed him more affection than since Ronnie'd been a little boy. In fact, there might even have been a tear in his eye.

Ronnie said, "Dad, that was one of your big meaning of life speeches ... and you weren't even wearing your special glasses."

"That only proves," said his dad, "that the dynamic of our relationship has changed forever."

"Do you want to come down and inspect what I did?"

"Nah," said his dad. "You're right. You've watched me often enough. Though ... I was kind of hoping for another fifteen minutes alone with the bitch. Something I didn't quite finish."

"Don't worry, Dad," said Ronnie. "I put it in the trash."

Maybe I shouldn't have let him know I know, Ronnie thought. His dad frowned; something flashed in his eyes. Was it anger, was it embarrassment? He wasn't sure. But then, all of a sudden, his dad was all smiles again. "Son," he said, "I've been so preoccupied with being a parent all these years ... you've really been my whole life. Do you think ... now that you're a senior ... you think I should start dating again?"

They chatted for a long time. Ronnie was amazed at his dad, who had always seemed so distant. It was as if they were making up for lost time. Or maybe squeezing in all the intimacy they should have shared now, quickly, before they would be forever lost to each other by the passing of time. They ate their breakfast off the same plate. Ronnie couldn't remember his dad ever doing that with him. This newfound closeness was so amazing to him that he almost forgot that he was in love, that a woman, reborn, was waiting for him, that soon they would be in each other's arms.

But all too soon, the front door chimed, and Ronnie knew that the first guests were arriving. When he heard that sound, his dad changed, abruptly became his old self. They didn't talk. Ronnie took the formal clothes from the closet and laid them at the foot of the bed, and left to let in the guests. He knew that his dad would only need ten minutes to go from his pajamas to the dark panoply of mourning.

The body had been on view for an hour; and now they were closing the lid and moving it into the chapel. Every funeral was pretty much the same; Ronnie had seen so many that they really made no impression on him. The relatives and friends, hushed and respectful or flamboyantly weeping ... the minister mouthing platitudes ... and always, the tasteless music. Ronnie sat in his black suit on a stool at the doorway, like an usher at a concert, trying to look solemn; inside, his mind was racing, his heart beating fast, waiting for the woman of his dreams to come to him.

He barely paid attention when the minister preached about the next world, or when Missy Cooper's fellow cheerleaders went up to the coffin and performed a little number they had been rehearsing the morning of her death. Where was Delbert? Where was the Lobster Lady?

He listened carefully. A hymn was starting up now. It was Amazing Grace. But he wasn't listening to the horrible organ playing, or the outoftune singing. He wanted to hear the latch on the door to the basement. At finally, faintly, he heard it click, heard footsteps ... uneven footsteps, the footsteps of a toddler just learning to walk. The hymn got louder. He stood up. He faced the twin tall vases with their silk roses, watching the passageway between two plaster columns that was the hidden entrance to the kitchen. The footsteps got a little closer. He heard someone stumble. He didn't move yet. He didn't dare believe in it. No. Not yet. Until the Lobster Lady stood there, her red dress trailing to the ground, sheer enough to reveal the outline of two shapely legs ... her red hair unpinned now, uncombed, falling across the curve of her bosom ... and the fragrance filled his nostrils ... and her eyes turned toward him with a look of gratitude and love ... and her red lips parted ... and silently mouthed his name.

He ran to her. She did not run, but tottered, regained her balance, was about to fall again, but he was there in time to catch her in his arms. They kissed.

"I promised," she said. "That you could make love to me. The real way. All the way."

"We can wait if you want," Ronnie said. "You're all one flesh now, all woman. We have our whole lives. We can be married first if you want."

"You know you can't wait," she said. "You're young, your blood is raging, you need to be inside me, you need to possess me. And what you've given me is nothing compared to the gift you're going to give me, Ronnie ... my beloved ... your innocence."

"I love you," he said again.

"Where's your bedroom?" she asked him.

He led her up the stairs. At the landing, looking down, he saw that Delbert was sitting in the chair he had vacated, watching them, waiting for the funeral to end.

He closed his bedroom door. He lit a candle, knowing how she loved candlelight, and drew the curtains, knowing how she hated the sun. How childish the room seemed now, with its athletic trophies, its Playboy pinup, its model airplanes, its plastic statue of Frankenstein's monster. Tomorrow he would burn all these relics of boyhood. Tomorrow was the beginning of a new life.

"Don't ... not for a minute," she said. "I want you to see me. I want you to really see me."

Then she undid a few buttons and stepped out of the crimson dress. It took his breath away. The join was perfect. The skin tones matched exactly. You couldn't tell where the Lobster Lady ended and Missy Cooper began. In the flickering light her body glowed, warm and infinitely desirable. He had touched her breasts before, but they seemed softer, more inviting. And then there was ... well ... that part of her ... underneath. Ronnie only knew the schoolyard words for it ... *pussy, cunt, box,* all ugly words ... and those scientific terms from sex ed, all as clinical as a thermometer. He wanted to be inside. He wanted to become ... what did the Bible call it? ... to become one flesh with her. Hurrying, he took off his mourning clothes, threw his black jacket on the floor, undid his tie, ripped the stiff shirt off his back, tore his boxers in his haste to be as naked as she was.

"Is this really want you want?" she said softly.

"Yes," he whispered.

"This is the act of love that will break my curse forever. Thank you for bringing me in from the outer darkness. Thank you for taking my pain upon yourself. You are my redeemer, my Jesus. I will always remember you."

"I don't want any more of this philosophizing," he said. He wanted to take charge. This was what his dad meant by becoming a man.

He threw himself on her. Enveloped her in his arms. She kissed him, teased at his nipples with her tongue, caressed his burgeoning erection with soft hands. And then, letting go, she moved toward the bed, laid down, propped up her head with a pillow, parted her new legs, and waited for him.

"Your friend does excellent work," she said.

"It's not just work," said Ronnie. "It's art."

"Art is illusion," she said. "A beautiful world can be only as deep as a layer of paint, and beneath it is only the rough canvas. A god on the surface; inside, cold, lifeless marble. Don't you wonder if I'm just a trick of the light, an accidental collage of texture and color that only seems to be a woman?"

"Don't be silly. You're no illusion," he said, as he climbed on top of her, as she guided him toward her moistening vagina with one hand.

"Don't you want to know what Delbert did with the rest of me?"

"I don't care," said Ronnie, as he plunged into the unknown.

"It's still inside me," said the Lobster Lady.

Vanilla Blood❧

Well, then. We might as well begin in the middle. Because the beginning has been done to death, hasn't it? The discovery of the bodies, the cross-country chase, even the allegations of police brutality ... you've seen it on CNN. Sixty Minutes. 20/20. Hard Copy. Graphic detail. You saw it all.

You saw her face. Pale as Ophelia in the bathtub of blood. The half-formed smile. The eyes, wide, emerald-green, the soggy blonde hair that wound about the corpse like a seaweed garnish; the skin, luminescent, of a piece with the porcelain she lay in; naked, of course, but they didn't show that on TV. If you were lucky, you caught the nudity when the camera lingered on the photos that first day on Court TV, marking the exhibits one by one, starting with the crime scene photographs.

You saw it; we can dispense with it.

You saw the perp on the cover of Newsweek. How young he looked! Anyone's kid, really — a nice Southern boy. Tried as an adult? You didn't really want to agree with the prosecutors — he seemed so goodlooking, so vulnerable, so — in need of a friendly social worker. Stared right through the camera and into your eyes … and into your heart.

Even the Pope sent a letter. As if that would have done much good here, right in the heart of Catholic-hating Klan country.

And then there was the lawyer. Pro bono, of course. A man who had been on every dream team in every high-profile trial in the last ten years. A talking head on Court TV. Once rendered Pat Buchanan speechless on Crossfire. He, too, had made the cover of Newsweek. But that was the "Superlawyers" cover story last year.

The prosecutor. An ice queen. Considered more robot than human … at least, until Flynt released the nude pics. You know this. You've spent whole watercooler breaks discussing her anatomy. Oh, yes, she was a natural redhead all right. Unless, of course, she had taken the trouble to dye … down there.

What a bitch! But an appealing one.

And the judge. He fumbled his way through the last big one, an eighteen month soap opera of celebrity murder, money, and sex. Now he had learned his lesson, and he was breathing fire, not taking any shit.

You are familiar with all these figures, I'm sure — there aren't many people in America who aren't. The Saturday Night Live parody alone said more than this brief memoir ever could.

So, instead, we'll start in the middle … just seconds after Judge Trepte kicked the cameras out of the courtroom.

We'll even go so far as to begin in the middle of a sentence.

— gone yet? Good, good.

— Sir? Get that thing out of my courtroom. Thank you. All the way out. When I kick out the cameras, sir, I kick out the cameras; I don't mean to have them lurking about in the anteroom. I mean, out, out, out.

— But, Your Honor, we've paid generously for the broadcast rights to — all right, Your Honor. Yes, sir. Goodbye, sir. Thank you, sir.

…

— and now, counselor, you will reveal to this court exactly why your next witness is arriving in so remarkable a fashion.

— He always travels this way, Your Honor.

— Objection! The defense is attempting to offer a corpse as a defense witness!

— You must admit, counselor, that the prosecution does have a point.

— He's not exactly dead, Your Honor. He just travels this way.

— In a coffin.

— Yes, Your Honor.

— Well, I'll be damned. Strike that. I think you will all agree that I made the right call in getting rid of the press. We can all relax now, and get to the bottom of this nonsense, without getting yet another lead story on the CBS Evening News. Miss Anderson, strike all that — all of it. This is not going to be a trial for the TV trial junkies. No. This is life and death ... some would add even undeath. Don't expect me to run this courtroom like Judge Itoh. More like Judge Dredd. Strike that too, Miss Anderson, strike, strike, strike, strike, strike. Now I'll stop pontificating and turn things over to you overpaid lawyers.

— The prosecution continues to object, Your Honor.

— Sustained.

— Your Honor, we cannot present this case without this witness's testimony.

— Then I will reconsider the objection when the witness deigns to get out of the coffin.

— He can't, yet. Your Honor. But I believe he will be able to in about five minutes....

Five minutes you may have. The court will recess for five minutes ... no, let's say ten. Some of us still smoke.

— Well, counselor?

— I don't understand it, Your Honor, but the witness doesn't appear to have stirred.

— Does the defense counsel propose to attempt to resuscitate the witness? We do have paramedics on call, do we not? Or will smelling salts do the trick?

— Your Honor, this has gone on far enough. Defense's sense of the theatrical is a little ill-timed, don't you think? I mean, they defend a few big name actors, they think they're Perry Mason. Can I continue to state my objection?

— Your objection stands. Bring on your next witness, counselor.

— We confess, Your Honor, we're sort of at a loss. In view of the apparent immobility of our star witness, we'd like to ... ah ... may I look at my notes? ... Jeremy Kindred. Yes. He's on the list.

— Very well.

— State your name for the record.

— Jeremy William Kindred.

— How old are you, Jeremy?

— I'm … I don't know exactly. Fifteen, sixteen.

— Are you a vampire?

— Yes.

— Are you a member of the group variously known as the Brotherhood of Blood, the Cult, the Vampire Society?

— I was, sir.

— You were?

— I was for a while, sir, but it was just what you'd call peer pressure, and no sir, I didn't kill nobody, didn't drink nobody's blood.

— Just answer the question, young man.

— Uh, sure, Your Honor.

— Tell us about it … in your own words, if you'd like.

— Objection! This is all irrelevant. The witness wasn't even at the killing. He's just wasting the jury's time.

— I think it's important to my case, Your Honor, that we clearly illustrate the circumstances under which these kids could come to believe that these crimes were not only acceptable, but desirable.

— Listen. The cameras are off, counselors. There's no more need for posturing. The jury is going to zone out completely unless you entertain them with a good story. So, kid, let's have it.

— Uh …

— You may proceed, Jeremy.

— Well, sir, I really joined it for the sex. I mean, there was a rumor that the Brotherhood had these orgies in the old Hanson house.

— That's an abandoned house?

— Yes, sir, by the cemetery. I don't why it ain't been tore down yet; it's kinda an eyesore. It's condemned, though. I always used to walk past it on my way to school. It's a big old place, creaky doors, peeling paint, scary statues of devils with leathery wings … and the big angel with the bronze sword … not shiny anymore, green mostly … not since the ringleaders of the Brotherhood was all put in jail. But that used to be the weirdest thing about that place. It was all crumbling and dirty except for that sword. That tall angel stood next to them wrought iron gates and it held its sword high in the air and the sword was all polished ... and you know, walking to school in winter, with the sun just rising, you could of swore that thing was on fire. The way it caught the sunlight. So the kids called it the Flaming Sword, like the preacher says about the Angel of Death. Anyways … there was this rumor that someone had wild parties there … you might call them raves, I guess … lotta E, lotta dope, lotta loose wenches if you know what I mean. So when Cat Sperling kept looking at me from the other end of the hall, she was a senior and all, with tits like balloons, you could say I was interested. Everyone knew that Cat had something to do with them parties. And everyone wanted that bitch, shit, even the girls wanted her. But there's something weird about her that you need to know. It wasn't no big Hollywood special effect kinda thing but … she carried the night around with her….

— Could you explain that a little more clearly, Jeremy? Take your time.

— Well, sir, it didn't matter if the sun was out, or if all the lights was on inside that school room. She always had like a shadow on her. Her skin was real pale, and it glimmered … well, like the moon was shining … but just on her you understand, just on her. There was a silvery thing about her eyes, too … you know like when you're in the woods all alone at night and you catch the moonlight dancing amongst the leaves … you catch my drift, sir?

— You're saying she was attractive. She had a unique look. Some kind of makeup, perhaps.

— Yeah well, it was like on no infomercial about pearly essence face cream … a lotta girls use that shit … she was different. It was like she was the real thing, and the others were all just imitating her. Did I tell you about the black hair? It was long, all the way to her waist. And she wore black lipstick. It matched.

— A goth, then.

— More than that. Like I said. Not a wannabe. The real thing.

— Objection, Your Honor, I fail to see how this catalog of feminine charms has any relevance whatsoever to the defense's case!

— Stop posturing, counselor. I've sent away the cameras; and the jury looks awake for the first time since this sorry spectacle began. I'm going to allow it. You may proceed, Mr. Kindred.

— Just tell the story in your own words, Jeremy.

— Well, I still think he's fishing, Your Honor.

— I've already overruled your objection.

— Jeremy?

— Yessir. Cat Sperling, sir.

— Cat Sperling let you know, through some kind of sign language or eye contact, that she had something to discuss with you.

— Not exactly, sir.

— What did she let you know?

— She wanted to fuck me, sir.

— Watch your language, young man! Try to act in a manner consistent with the dignity and majesty of the law — what's left of it!

— I'm sorry, Your Honor; I don't know no other word for what she was trying to say.

— Very well, then. The court will take into account the deprived environment you clearly come from.

— I ain't no trailer trash, Your Honor!

— Quite so, young man, quite so. Why don't you finish telling your story to the court?

— Sure, Your Honor. Like I said, I got the Look from her. There ain't no mistaking the Look, sir. From all the way across the hall, and I knew she wanted me. Well, so there's a place you go to when you give someone the Look … at least that's how it works at Edward Kramer High. The place is up on a hill, you know, the hill just north of the cemetery. There's a road that winds up, and a hiking trail as well. At Kramer, we don't need to pass notes; it's a tradition; you get the Look, and if you give the Look back, then you go meet on the hill. If you hold up one finger, it means tonight; two fingers means we'll set a time later. Well, Cat held up one finger; everyone saw it, even if they didn't say nothing; Kramer ain't a kiss and tell kind of a school.

— It's an ancient tradition, then.

— I'd say so, sir.

— One that your parents would know about. That even a few members of this jury may well have experienced, if they happened to have gone to your high school.

— Did Cat Sperling meet you on the hill that night?

— Yes, sir.

— Did she then proceed to initiate you into the Brotherhood of Blood?

— Oh, no, sir. You can't get in just like that.

— Tell the court what happened, Jeremy.

— Well, that night, I went up to the hill. I borrowed my Mom's Malibu. I don't have a license, but you said I'd have immunity, right?

— This is a multiple murder case, Jeremy. I don't think the court is too worried about your license.

— Okay, okay. Well, she was waiting there all right. She was every bit as enticing as the rumors said. It was windy and her hair was flying every which way … and catching the moonlight. She leaned against a tree with a joint in one hand … I can say that, can't I? … and her eyes were wild. I couldn't believe my luck. I mean, to tell you the truth, I'd never done it before. Unless you count, one time, in summer camp —

— That's all right, Jeremy. I don't think the court needs an exegesis of your sexual experiences.

— Okay. So she says to me, Jeremy Kindred, I've had my eye on you. You're a good-looking kid. And I says, Yeah, they say that. I'm tall for my age, almost six feet already. And she says, You got that unplucked look. Like a glistening round apple in a tree … a fresh smell, apple-scented shampoo maybe, a little-kid smell in a big-kid body … and I know how much you want me, seen how you stare at me in across the hallway or last week when we had that big assembly with the Yankee AIDS speaker. Here, take a drag of this, it'll relax you, I know your heart's pounding, boy. Really pull on it, hard I mean hard. Come closer. You always wanted to touch them, didn't you? Here. Put your hand on them. Through the sweater for now, I ain't no whore … I know you like it, Jeremy Kindred. So well, I felt them titties and they were fine. Firmer than I thought they'd be. Fairly straining against the wool they was. Got a rise out of me, lemme tell you. It was something to be alone on the hill with Cat Sperling. It sure turned my head. I didn't even think nothing of it when she asked for a drop of blood.

— So let me get this straight, Jeremy. This woman, this older woman —

— She won't but three years older than me, sir, if that! —

— Well, for the sake of argument, a slightly older and certainly much more sophisticated woman … lures you to a well-known trysting spot … gets you all hot and bothered … and suddenly asks to drink your blood?

— She didn't say drink, sir. You're jumping the gun on the story. She just said, Jeremy, you cute-as-a-button boytoy, let me have a drop of blood. The drinking didn't rightly occur to me, not at that moment … I don't know what was occurring to me, really, excepting I wanted to get inside her jeans something fierce. I knew she was a member of that Brotherhood thing, so blood had to figure in it somewhere … like swearing blood-brotherhood with your best buddy in junior high or something. Well, she asked for a drop of blood, and by now we were in the back seat of the Malibu, I forgot to say that, didn't I? … and I was reaching into her jeans … it didn't feel down there like I thought it would … more leathery … and slick … like a beat-up old wallet. And she was all, I have a needle here, and I just need a little bit, just a thimbleful would do the trick right fine. And she reached into a back pocket and pulled out a hypodermic. The needle glinted in the moonlight that reflected off the rear view mirror and you know what it made me mighty hard, more than I'd ever felt before in my life, cause I guess there was something dark about it, something forbidden ... and this was how she did it … she yanked my pants down to my knees and kinda crouched down and pushed me up into her, and at the same time she jabbed that needle into my chest, like she was fixing to impale my heart. Well, I can't tell you how that made feel, I mean, I just about burst right then and there, after being inside of her only a minute … and then I thought, well, I'm screwed for sure, because Cat Sperling ain't gonna want a green kid who can't last but a minute inside the famousest pussy in town.

— Your Honor, I simply have to object. I just don't see how this catalog of adolescent fumbling can possibly relate to the defense's case.

— If you'd bear with me for a second, Your Honor, I believe the witness is about to reach a crucial point of evidence in the defense's case … the blood.

— All right, counselor. But if you don't reach some kind of relevance within the next two minutes —

—Jeremy, tell the court about what happened next.

— Well, sir, she didn't seem to pay no mind to the fact that I come inside her. She was only interested in the blood. When she saw that stream of red gushing into that syringe, she started thrashing and heaving and carrying on something fierce. She was all moaning, too … and shrieking … like a passel of cats in a back alley. I never seen anything like it, sir, and I've watched a lot of pornos. And then she's all shuddering to a climax right there in the back seat of my Malibu. And the blood's dribbling from her lips … but it's not a scary thing … it's warming her, lighting up her face … her cheeks were pale before, but now they're all blushing just a bit. And then she says to me, I want you to join. Join what? I asks her, but I already know what she means. I said, I heard there's a lotta parties, and in them parties you all get down, if you know what I mean. Parties right in the cemetery's what I heard. She smiled. You're coming to the very next one, she says, and it's on Friday the Thirteenth … next weekend … but it'll probably last until Sunday morning … when some of us, the ones that aren't in too deep, who can still stand the vibes, why, we go to church. I'm thinking that it can't be that bad if they go to church afterwards. So I say, sure, I'll come. And she says, Be sure and bring your best friend Jody.

— Who did she mean by that?

— Jody Palmer, my best friend.

— The defendant?

— Yes sir, he sure is.

— I trust the prosecution is now satisfied as to the relevance of this witness?

— We continue to object, Your Honor. All this is fascinating in a prurient sort of way … I can see the reporter from CBS in the back there, desperately looking for an opening to demand the cameras back … but the fact remains that Jody Palmer killed several people, including his mother … and that he's being tried for murder.

— Your Honor, we must have some latitude here. The prosecution's perfectly aware that we're trying to establish that the defendant was under such crippling social and emotional pressure that he believed he no longer had a choice. You must allow the witness to —

— Your Honor! The coffin lid is shaking!

— Well, hold it down, bailiff!

— I can't! There's something inside … struggling to get out!

— Jesus Christ, I forgot Daylight Savings Time! Sunset's an hour later!

— Cut the profanity, counselor.

— I'm sorry, Your Honor, but —

— I'm fining you a thousand dollars for contempt. Get your checkbook out this minute, counselor. Bailiff! Control that coffin!

— Blast! The lid's off!

— Well, put it back on.

— It's fighting back! Someone's inside — and he — she — it's trying to sit up!

— Well, restrain him, bailiff.

— It's a woman, Your Honor … a young woman.

— Cat!

— The witness will refrain from speaking unless it is in response to a question from counsel, or from myself.

— Oh. Yes, Your Honor. Yes, sir. I didn't mean to —

— Counsel for the defense … you've been referring to this witness in the masculine gender from the beginning. And now that your witness has deigned to emerge from her … ah … conveyance, she appears to be very, very feminine indeed. Exceptionally so, and flaunting it besides. Do you always instruct your witnesses to appear in court in flimsy negligees? Is this a courtroom or a Frederick's of Hollywood catalogue? For God's sake, madam, cover yourself! Bailiff … a cloak for the witness. I won't have the jury distracted by her endowments. In fact, I won't have the jury distracted at all; counsel, I want an explanation.

— Your Honor, could we have a brief sidebar? This isn't the witness we had in mind for this portion of the testimony. There appears to have been a … misunderstanding.

— Oh, Jeremy … you sure are a sight! You look real small and scared and powerless up there in that witness box. But it's okay, baby. Cat's here now. Cat will hold your hand. It's gonna be all right. You didn't do nothing wrong … and it's not you that's on trial.

— But Cat … you're dead! I saw you die!

— Death ain't nothing, baby. Just another kind of doorway. And there's more than one way of going through that doorway … you can let them shove you through, and you can let them flush the key down the toilet bowl of eternity … or you can wrest that key out of their hand and take it with you … so they can't slam the door in your face … so you can live forever on the edge of life and death … I did it, baby, just like I said I would … I did it, baby. Oh, yes, I crossed over, and I crossed back. Just like the duke said. And you can do it too. Don't be afraid, Jeremy. Oh, and Mr. Counsel … the duke says he's sorry, but he can't be in court tonight. Something's come up. He sent me instead. I can give all the evidence you need.

— The duke, as you call him, Miss … Sperling, is it? … is under subpoena.

— Subpoenas don't work too good on dead people, Mr. Judge. If the duke wants to come to your court, he'll come; but your laws don't really apply to him. The undead have their own laws. There's nothing in the constitution about them.

— On the contrary, Ms. Sperling. Just because creatures you're calling the undead are not specifically mentioned in law doesn't make them outside the law at all. Anyone who is evidently capable of rational discourse and capable of appearing here and making remarks, relevant or otherwise, is a prima facie candidate for personhood and I can damn well hold them in contempt if I so choose!

— Your Honor, the witness is ... well ... she's sort of swirling, melting into some kind of mist … and now there's a black cat running around the courtroom … it doesn't seem very friendly, sir …in fact, it's got poor Mrs. Coates trying to climb up one of the pillars … it could be rabid, Your Honor.

— Shoot the critter! I won't have any more disruptions!

— Sir, the cat appears to have leapt out of the window.

— That's four stories, bailiff! Surely even a cat can't leap for stories and survive … now what? It's flying into the night? You see great leathern wings against the face of the full moon, bailiff? Is this Batman or is it a court of law? Put that camera away, Mr. Prinze, or I'm kicking CNN out completely. And I'm hereby instructing the jury to ignore all of this — the woman climbing out of the coffin, the soap-opera dialogue between Ms. Sperling and the witness, the bizarre metamorphosis from female to feline, and Mrs. Coates's screams. None of this ever happened, do you hear? None of it!

— Your Honor …

— What is it now, counselor? My patience is wearing pretty thin.

— In view of the fact that we have let the wrong … ah, cat out of the bag, and in view of the fact that the witness currently on the stand hasn't yet completed his testimony….

— Quite, quite, counselor. I think there's been quite enough claptrap for one day. Court will reconvene tomorrow at nine o'clock sharp, corpses and all.

— The corpse … and I will try to make sure we have the right one on hand tomorrow, Your Honor … will not actually be able to say anything until sundown … might an allowance be made? Please don't consider it contempt; consider it rather to be a medical condition that prevents the witness from testifying during daylight hours.

— All right. I'm going to give you a lot of leeway, counselor. But any cats, bats, or talking corpses are going to have to abide by my rules. Court will reconvene at three p.m, then — we will allow the current witness to finish his touching story — by which time sundown will have arrived and we will be able to continue with your key witness — assuming him, or her, to have completed his, or her beauty sleep at that time.

❧

— So, Jeremy … having had your blood sipped by the sexiest girl at Kramer High in what can only be described as a somewhat erotic experience … did you then accept Ms. Sperling's invitation to an event which you believed would be some kind of wild, gothic, orgy?

— Yes, sir.

— And did you bring the defendant with you on that occasion?

— Uh, yes, sir.

— And did you and the defendant drink blood at that event?

— Yes, sir. Vanilla.

— Vanilla?

— When the new ones drink blood for the first time … they mix it with vanilla syrup. Kinda kills the taste. Gets you used to it. It's like, uh, you wouldn't give your kid brother a straight shot of JD the first time, not without mixing it with a Coke or something. He'll get just as drunk, but it won't burn his throat as bad.

— What did you tell the defendant to get him to come to this event?

— Oh, that was easy. Jody's a big vampire fan. He watches vampire movies all the time, and he plays roleplaying games, live-action ones, too. Last year, we hitchhiked down to some sci-fi convention in Chattanooga, and he got into a live-action vampire thing that lasted the whole weekend, 24/7. He didn't even try to pick up no bitches or get fucked up, he was so caught up in the game. See, when it came to Cat Sperling's big event, orgy, whatever you wanted to call it, I was just looking to get laid, but Jody wanted something deeper. When I told him that she'd asked me to bring him, asked for him by name even, he got all glassy-eyed and weird, and he was all, "Finally. This is it. The call. The embrace of ultimate darkness." Which sounds like the script of a video game, but he said it all like it was for real. Jody has these deep eyes, that cornflower blue color, you know, that the bitches like so much; he could have had bitches, except he wouldn't play any of the games they wanted him to play. So when he starts talking about ultimate darkness, and he puts on this weird, toneless kind of voice, like he's, I don't know, possessed or something, it gets creepy. That's why the kid had no friends. He scared people. Even so, I wouldn't exactly call him guilty of murder.

— Objection! The witness is speculating wildly about the defendant's guilt … even without counsel calling for such speculation. He's not here to speak to these issues.

— Yes, yes. The jury will disregard that, of course; the defendant's guilt is for the jury to decide, not this benighted young man. Please confine your testimony to the facts, Mr. Kindred … if any.

— All right, Jeremy. You do understand what the judge is saying, right? Just tell us what happened. No opinions, just facts.

— Yessir.

— You passed on Cat Sperling's invitation to the defendant.

— Yes.

— How did you convince the defendant to attend?

— I told him it was the wildest live action role playing game of all time.

— You didn't mention the … erotic element?

— Oh, yes, sir. I told him there would be an orgy.

— And how did he react to that?

— He said, you can have the sex, Jeremy, long as I can have the violence.

— So is it fair to say that the defendant had a tendency towards violence?

— He was just kidding, sir! I never knew Jody to harm a flea, except in some fantasy or game, and then, of course, he'd go crazy … ripping off heads or wrapping himself in entrails … you know, movie special effects kind of shit. But in real life, no sir, Jody was gentle. I've seen him walk sideways so he wouldn't step on a bug. Most guys kinda enjoy stepping on bugs … taking a life, you know, even if it's just a bug's life. Jody wasn't like that. Loner, though. At lunch, he'd always be by himself, because even though I'm his best friend, you didn't want to be seen hanging around with a loser; he understood that; we only hung together after school, or at the mall. But even sitting by himself, munching on them power bars which was all he ever had packed for his lunch, he had an audience … there was always bitches eying him from a distance, wanting him. I guess it was the eyes. That's why he was on the cover of Time, wasn't it? The eyes. I assumed that's why Cat wanted me to bring him. And I know he's been getting a lot of mail from bitches all around the country, since that magazine cover; he told me that one time when they let me visit him in jail. I thought he'd be more, you know, fucked up by jail, what with all them big dudes named Bubba, but he says ain't none of them touched him; they're all scared of him. It's been put out that he has powers, you know, going through keyholes, transforming into bats, and all that vampire movie shit; but what I wanna know is, if that's true, why hasn't he escaped from jail? Well okay, I guess I'm getting off the subject again. You wanna know about the party in the cemetery, the Friday the Thirteenth thing …

and how my friend Jody come to be accused of wiping out his family and a passel of his friends.

— Yes, Jeremy. Take your time. I know some of this is painful. But the jury needs to get the whole picture.

— Where was I?

— Perhaps you could go back to the vanilla blood.

— Yeah. It was like a cocktail almost. They served it in tall cone-shaped glasses, flutes they called them; champagne comes the same way, I heard tell. When me and Jody got there, it was close to midnight. That's because Jody took some convincing, even though he loved vampires; these weren't his kind of people. Leastways, we assumed that it would be mostly the school Goth crowd, the Nine Inch Nails types, the Anne Rice readers; actually it was kinda surprising who was there. It wasn't even confined to kids from Kramer High. I mean, Miss Higginbotham, the social studies teacher, was there ... and she was bare-ass nekkid, and lying on top of a big old gravestone with her hippo-sized haunches in the air ... and moaning. And this ... well, this black dude was all on her shit, and he won't wearing nothing but a pair of black leather Pampers, and a nose ring the size of a golf ball, which must have tickled old Higginbotham's clit something fierce ... well, she was moaning every time his head bobbed up and down, and her titties were flapping around like a couple of beached flounders. Shit she was a sight, all moaning and wet in the moonlight like that. And there were other people scamming against grave markers; some guy was even trying to pork the stone angel that guards the cemetery gate. And there was this girl I'd never seen before, passing around the glasses, I mean flutes, filled with vanilla blood, and that was the only food they had at the whole party, if you can call it food. Well, just about everyone seemed occupied with someone else, and no one paid much mind to me and Jody, and the only one who said anything to us was the girl with the tray of blood; she stopped to ask us if we were new, and when we said yes, she told us drink up, it's real important for the new ones to drink up, can't really be part of the action until you've taken the first step; so we did.

— What sensation did you associate with drinking this, ah, "vanilla blood"?

— Hey, I don't rightly know if I should tell you what it was really like — this being a court of law and all.

— You're under oath, Jeremy. And also, you have immunity.

— So you can't use nothing I say against me? Nothing at all?

— Well — no.

— Objection! The witness only has use immunity.

— I'll sustain that, but I want to hear the witness's answer.

— Jeremy, the judge isn't going to do anything to you for what you say. He just wants to hear your answer.

— Well, sir, did you ever try E?

— Are you saying that the effects of this "vanilla blood" were somewhat akin to the drug E — Ecstasy — a drug popular among the "rave" segment of the student population?

— Well, if I answered that, I'd have to say that I'd used E before, and the judge just sustained that mean-looking bitch's objection. So I'll just say it gave me a boner the size of a baseball bat, and I wanted to screw the first thing I saw.

— Which was?

— Objection! Irrelevant.

— Actually, Your Honor, this answer speaks directly to the defendant's motivation.

— All right, I'll allow the question, but you'd better proceed very quickly to something important. Or the gentleman from CNN is liable to wet his pants.

— Jeremy, and what was the first thing you saw that you wanted to, as you so delicately put it, screw?

— Well, this is kinda embarrassing, sir. I mean, I wouldn't want you to think I'm gay or nothing, but I was so horny I wanted to do Jody … well, okay, there was something about him, the eyes, or whatever, anyway, on Brother Thompson's Christian summer camp last year, we all learned about circle jerks from the brother himself, so it wasn't like …

— Order in the court!

— And I mean, people were going crazy in that graveyard. I swear, I saw Mr. Smith, the football coach, getting boned up the butt by Mr. Oliver, who's like a police sergeant down at —

— Order in the goddamn court!

— Your Honor, we're not here to discuss the sexual antics of half the town. Could the witness confine himself to —

— Brother Thompson was even there, and he was handcuffed to a gravestone, and these motorcycle bitches were prodding him with cigarettes, and he was all moaning.

— That's enough, Mr. Kindred. Counselor, instruct your witness to get to the point.

— So, Jeremy, you, ah, made a pass at your best friend.

— Well, not exactly. It was more like this: I swallowed a couple of mouthfuls of that blood cocktail thing, and everything went all misty … well, okay, and I felt like my veins were on fire … like this burning sensation, this tingling, everywhere, especially, you know, down there … and the next thing I knew, I was on Jody's leg, like a dog or something, rubbing myself up and down on it. But he wasn't getting horny off that blood at all. It wasn't affecting him the same way. Even though there was couples, threesomes, getting down every which way, in the light of the moon, with a dark, pounding music pouring out of a ghettoblaster somewhere … like one of them imperial orgy scenes in Caligula, you know? … Jody wouldn't have none of it. He shook me off of him like you'd shake off, well, a dog. — "Don't," he said. "You're like all them others. To me the blood feels different. I think maybe I ain't the same kind as you, maybe I don't belong with the likes of you. What you're all doing seems so empty to me. Blood sings a different music to me. When I look into the dark, I look right past all of you and all your sleazy thrills, your wannabe games, I see you all just flirting with the darkness … not willing to embrace it … to become a part of it … no, you're not like me after all, and it makes me sad because you've been a good friend to me, Jeremy, all these years when no one would talk to me because I'm like the school outcast, the mutant in the hallway … today I'm starting to learn who I really am."

— So the defendant had, as it were, an epiphanic moment from the drinking of human blood?

— I don't rightly know what that means, sir.

— Doesn't matter. That evening changed him, didn't it?

— Maybe so. What he said to me, though, was he found his true self.

— And his true self was what? A vampire?

— Won't that simple, sir. But anyways, I didn't have time to listen to him ranting on at that point, because, as I said, I was thinking with my dick. And soon my dick found something to play with. There was this mousy girl, no one anyone would look at twice in the daylight … her name was Constance Thorpe … and the only time I ever spent more than five seconds in her company was when me and her was paired off cutting up rats in biology lab one time. You know, she always used to make me nervous. She had nerd glasses, and she had a way of pulling out them rat intestines that made it look like she was enjoying it too much. And she dressed like a refugee from the 60s, parents must've been hippies or something and she forgot to rebel. Well I saw her leaning against a tombstone and she wasn't the same bitch at all, lemme tell you. She'd lost the glasses and she even had a spot of makeup on. But I didn't really give a shit, because of whatever it was in that blood; all I cared about was that she made a beeline for me and kinda nosedived toward my crotch. Before you knew it she'd unzipped me and she was all up on me like a noisy old vacuum cleaner. I mean, I wouldn't have been seen dead with her normally, but you should have seen her suck, I mean, that girl could suck. She was wild, too, licking up a storm on my balls and even thrusting down past them, I think she'd have stuck it up my butt if my pants had come all the way down, but the zipper was all tangled in her hair. Must've hurt, it yanking on that hair like that, sir, but she sucked with a will, like her life depended on it. So I sorta leaned back against the gravestone, closed my eyes, and slipped into like a kind of trance, just letting myself go with the flow of it … then I sort of came too with a shock because I could feel this pinprick, this sharp pain that wouldn't go away. I looked down and she had pulled out a syringe and she'd stuck me right in the shaft, and you know how much blood gets down there when you got a boner. I guess I kinda panicked, even though I knew that these people have a thing about blood, and I drew back, and well, I knocked the syringe out and I jizzed at the same time, and there was blood and cum everywhere … well, Constance was going crazy now, lapping up everything, sperm, blood, sweat, I could have pissed on her face and she'd've drunk it. Holy shit! I didn't like it. The high of the vanilla blood was coming down now. I was all dizzy. This wasn't how I thought it would feel. I felt all dirty inside. That's when I decided to go looking for Jody. I sorta pushed Constance out of the way. She was on all fours, the fucking nympho bitch, and already sniffing for a fresh piece of meat to chew on. I kept calling Jody's name, asked a couple people where he was, and they kept shrugging or being too involved with their own shit.

— And where did you in fact discover the defendant to be?

— Well, I'm getting to that, sir!

— Good. I see that the prosecution has become too, ah, involved in its prurient fascination with the material to object any further....

— There's no need for the defense to snipe, Your Honor, when it is clearly burying itself with every word this so called witness utters.

— Be that as it may … Mr. Kindred?

— Okay. Well, there's this big old structure bang in the middle of the cemetery, see, and it's the oldest monument there. I think it dates to long before the war.

— You mean the Civil War.

— Yes, sir.

— I think most of the jury are familiar with the monument you're referring to. It's the Forbin-St.Cloud Memorial, right? Built by a prominent French family, in the days when our little city was booming. Which times, since the banning of hemp cultivation, are long past. A bizarrely incongruous Gothic monstrosity, surrounded by a wrought iron fence with strange-looking gargoyles on top, rumored to have underground passageways, under whose sheltering eaves the homeless of this town often rest, as the local police force rarely bothers to kick them out, rarely even patrols this area because of the mysterious death of Police Sergeant McKinley, found garroted and disemboweled and spread-eagled over the —

— Why is the defense now regaling us with a history lesson, Your Honor? Objection!

— I'll stop, Your Honor. I just thought the local color would be helpful. The Forbin-St. Cloud monument has … vibes. I want the jury to understand that. Since all of them heard the ghost stories when they were kids, and few were brave enough to go there. I know the prosecution is anxious to get back to the dirty bits. So how about it, Mr. Kindred? Let's have 'em. The dirty bits.

— Like I said, sir, I thought I saw the back of Jody's head, and he was squeezing through the iron bars into the Fo-for- … well, we don't call it that, sir.

— What do you call it?

— We call it the Hellhouse.

— Why?

— Well, sir, on account of … it's big enough to be a house, what with all the underground passages it's supposed to have … and it's got this entranceway … well, a fake entranceway … that looks like the mouth of hell … a big old demon's jaw in stone with a stone door that can't be opened. Well … I didn't think it could be opened. But then … I saw Jody sort of standing there … at the stone mouth … you could see the sculpted flames of hell there … and he was just standing there. Just staring. Like he'd seen something … supernatural. Well, I kind of snuck up behind him. I guess I startled him because when he felt me breathing down his neck he screamed up a storm. I mean he had like a panic attack, and I hadn't never seen him lose his cool before. I got him calmed down. I kept saying, it ain't so bad, Jody, nothing bad's happened yet, maybe we just lost a bit of blood is all. Maybe we're a bit weak from that, you know, dizzy, seeing things. When you lose blood you see things. We learned that in school. But he was all, I saw what I saw. I said, What did you see? and he said, Nothing. Fucking nothing, and don't ask me again. I ain't crazy. I said, Nobody said you was. Just tell me what you seen there.

— And did the defendant respond?

— Yeah.

— What did he say?

— He more than said, sir. Well at first he just murmured, They went through the doorway, they just up and walked right on through there like it was air, I can feel them inside there, feel the heat of their souls inside the dead empty space … but pretty soon he was a-banging on that stone with his fists, like he should have been able to melt right through it. Well, what do you know? The wall started to give.

— He shattered a mausoleum wall with his fists?

— Not hardly, sir. I mean the wall and him seemed to kind of meld together, and he was sort of sinking into it.

— What did you do, Jeremy?

— I thought he was going to die. I mean, getting sucked into a jello kind of a wall, it was one of them Poltergeist-style special effects, like you see in movies. So I guess I grabbed on to him, and that's how I ended up getting pulled inside too. The stone felt mushy. Oily, you know. It made my flesh crawl. But the wall closed right up again as soon as we got through, and it was dark as shit in there, and won't no way to get back out. I almost shat my pants, I don't mind telling you, sir, it was that scary. The air was all moist and stale-smelling. I don't know how dead people are supposed to smell, but I could feel death there. Well, after a time, you could start to see a bit of light. Water was dripping. Where we were was a kind of corridor leading downward. And we heard voices. From down below. I was shaking, sir. And then Jody said the strangest thing. He said, Jer, we been buddies for a long time, but there's places you weren't meant to go … places I have to go alone. You weren't meant to pass through to this place, but you held on to me, and maybe that's good, because if anything ever happens to me, you can bear witness one day, you can speak the truth about me, shout it out, even if nobody ever believes you, or even understands what you say. I ain't long for this world, Jer, but I'm meant to go out like a comet, not like a lil old candle. You know that, don't you? I've always been different … like everyone's born facing the same way, their butts to the past, their faces to the future, but not me, I go sideways, past and future are a sidestream to me, a path I can never tread.

— Quite a speech for a teenager, don't you think?

— Objection! Calls for speculation.

— Ah, I see that the Madame Prosecutor has awakened. Sustained.

— That's all right, Your Honor, I was only being rhetorical. Mr. Kindred … Jeremy … I'll say it a different way. Did your friend, the defendant, often make long speeches like that?

— Not often. But more than any other kid I knew. If he got going, he could talk up a storm. Almost like a preacher, except it would be all about violence and death and dark things.

— Are you aware that the defendant hasn't said a word since he was taken into custody?

— I've heard that, sir.

— So he's definitely changed.

— Yes, sir. He ain't human no more.

— Literally?

— Well, sir, I was getting to that.

— Proceed.

— Well, like I said, there was voices. And the corridor leading downward. And the light, you see, the light came from down below. A flickering, red light, kind of like the flames of hell I guess. And even though Jody told me, No, you stay up here, this is for me alone … well, I guess I couldn't help following him down there. I was curious, sure. But it was also creepy as shit, and I didn't want to be alone.

— Did the defendant know you were following him?

— Sort of. But you see, he was like in his own world. He really didn't pay me no mind at all. I was like a puppy dog or something … no, a shadow more like, a nothing.

— To whom did the voices belong?

— Well okay, we kept going down deeper and deeper, because the corridor ended in steps and the steps led us deeper and deeper underground. Maybe we were going into the hillside, I don't know; I lost my sense of direction. Because now there were steps going up, and passageways leading sideways. It as like that story we learned in Mrs. Seymour's class one time, the one with the maze and the bullheaded man and the hero with his ball of yarn. The walls glowed. It was a cold light, millions of dots of light, you know, like you get in caves sometimes, phosphorescence I think it's called. I followed. After what seemed like a long time, it widened into a cave. I think it was part natural, this cave, but there was also a bunch of marble columns and statues of weeping angels and other cool gothic shit. The light came from flaming torches on the walls. Some parts of the walls had paintings, Egyptian stuff, guys with dog's heads, other parts had been painted over. It was all coated with soot, and when the torches flickered, it looked like them pictures was moving. And at the far end, there were niches in the wall, and in the niches were dead people. I mean some were long dead, like skeletons, but some were fresh … and some of them I recognized. I mean, they went to my school. I mean, they weren't supposed to be dead at all. I mean, I would have heard of it if they'd died, I was in some of the same classes. Well, I wasn't that sure. Like I said, I was dizzy. And the sex thing hadn't totally worn off. I hid behind a big statue. An angel. The archangel Michael, I think, with a flaming sword. The sword was metal and sort of attached to his hand with a leather thong. And a bronze cross around his neck. His wings were wide enough that I could crouch down and peep through a little chink where his elbow lifted up against his robe. Apart from the sword and the cross he was all marble, and cold. And well, I wasn't dressed for the cold, so I was shivering as I huddled there, trying not to breathe too much.

— What did the defendant do at that point?

— He stood there, in a semicircle of light, facing all of them dead folks, and I saw there was three coffins laying there, fine old coffins made of carved wood with all gold on them. The coffins are just laying there, and the middle one, the grandest one of them all, is closed, but the other two have their lids on the ground next to them and they're empty, you see. And there's people here. They're hard to see at first, because they're all blended with the shadows, and it takes me a while to make them out. They ain't the same kind of people as the ones in the orgy up there in the cemetery grounds. They're, well, pale looking. What was that word for the way the walls was all glowing? Phosphorescent. Yeah. That was in their faces, too. When you looked at one of them a long time you could see the cold light clinging to their faces. They all wore black. I don't mean all Dracula capes and stuff. I mean, some of them had capes, but there were clothes from olden times, and clothes you could see down at the Goth coffee house over in the next town. There was leather and fishnet stockings. There was black lipstick. Sunken eyes. Some had sweeping robes, you know, the kind that rustle when you walk. And well, standing next to one of the empty coffins was Cat Sperling, and she was totally naked. And by the other coffin was … shit man, it's weird to think of it now, but it was Constance Thorpe, the little geek that done went down on me next to that gravestone up above. She was naked, too. She looked better than I thought she would. I couldn't believe it. The only two bitches I'd ever really messed around with, and they were standing around bare-ass naked in front of a bunch of ghouls in black. I gotta admit, it was making me, you know, all hot down there all over again. I watched my friend Jody. They didn't seem to notice him at first, them two girls, because they were busy staring into each other's eyes. I mean, I thought I was trapped inside of a lesbo porno. I mean, this was fucking wild. I never dreamed them two would have a thing for each other, I mean, the sexiest girl at Kramer High and some gap-toothed nerd with a thing for cutting up mice and frogs … secretly wanting to dyke it out? … I could see it in their eyes. Cat went without saying, but Constance looked different. A glow in her flesh. Gleaming. Maybe it was sweat. She had hard little nipples. They were inching toward each other. I was all, Holy shit, they're gonna get it on right here, in front of all these people … if they even are people. Cat's upper lip was quivering. The sweat was beading up on it. I could barely look at their pussies. I'd glimpsed pussy before, and in pornos you watch it all you want, but it's on a TV screen. This was different. I was afraid if I stared too long, I don't know, I was gonna have an accident.

— Your Honor, could the witness get to the point already?

— Sustained.

— I'm afraid he's right, Jeremy. The jury doesn't really need to know about your … accidents.

— Well, I didn't have no accident anyways, sir.

— Why?

— Just when I thought the two of them were going to really, you know, get down, the lid of the coffin in the middle started to creak open.

— A little like yesterday's little incident?

— Oh, no, sir. It was real slow, like. And then all the people there fell on the floor. I don't mean they tripped, I mean they fell to their knees, faces in the dust, even the two naked bitches. It was like, you know, I seen this movie about an ancient Chinese emperor, it was death to look him directly in the face. I could feel … fear in the room … and power. Real power. I was scared. I narrowly avoided one kind of accident, and now I was fixing to have another kind. Well, the lid was creaking open. Dust was flying. The lid swung up and this old man was sitting up slowly. He was old, real old. Okay, he didn't look that old, but you could feel it in him. And he spoke. Slowly. Like he was having trouble remembering how to speak. Later they done told me that his kind don't have much use for talking amongst themselves; it's chiefly for the benefit of the ones that are still human. Oh, it won't English neither. But one of the guys in black got up off his knees and crept up closer, and he translated everything in a flat, echoey voice. The first thing he says is, The Duke asks what new creatures come before him today.

— Meaning the two girls?

— Yes, sir, I guess, because the sex goddess and the geek stand up, and they're all coyly looking at the floor and half-smiling, and their nipples are still hard. And they both say, Your Grace, we humbly beg for the honor of attending you. Well, his Grace mumbles something, and the translator says, How may you prove your worthiness? And they answer, We are yours entirely, body, soul, in life and death and undeath. We wish to become consorts of the darkness. We wish the everlasting night. We pine for the sunset. We abhor the light. We have listened in the wilderness and heard the music of the night.

— The sex goddess and the geek, as you call them, said all that? In those precise words?

— I reckon it was learned from a book or something, sir.

— So this appeared to be some kind of ritual?

— Yes, sir.

— Your Honor, I thought that this trial was about the defendant, not the erotic fantasies of some disturbed adolescent. I must continue to protest this undignified latitude in allowing endless filth to spew forth from the witness without any real connection to the defendant's guilt or innocence!

— Yes, yes, sustained, sustained, though I'm sure the lurid details will all be in your next book, counselor!

— I resent that, Your Honor!

— Be quiet and let the kid tell the rest of his story. If the defense would care to continue … I'm as anxious to get to the relevance of this as anyone else here.

— Yes, Your Honor. Mr. Kindred … Jeremy … go on. Go easy on the sex. Unless it specifically concerns the defendant.

— All right, sir.

— Tell us about the defendant and his role in all this, then.

— Well, the translator guy, he says to the two girls, You know that before you can cross over, you must bid the flesh farewell … and you must find a willing lamb … a sacrifice. And Cat Sperling said, We have such a lamb, Your Grace. We've tracked him, we've lured him, we've cornered him, and we have him.

— And by "him", they meant the defendant?

— I guess so, sir, cause Jody done stepped forward.

— What was the defendant's demeanor?

— Huh?

— How did he look?

— Pale, sir, real pale. But determined, too. Whatever was about to happen, it looked like he'd thought it over and was gonna do it, no matter what. Grim, sir, real grim. It's amazing to me how young he looks at that moment. I know he's really older than me, but he comes off like a little kid. Scrawny. And so pale. Maybe that phosphorescence shit was rubbing off on him. He looked back only once. Looked me right in the eye. Knew I was there, knew I was watching. No one else saw, no one else knew. I thought about what he said to me earlier. I ain't long for this world, Jer, but I'm meant to go out like a comet, not like a lil old candle. Jody was fixing to die. I realized that. All of a sudden. Something had happened between him and Cat Sperling. Something that had pushed him over the edge. Like the preacher says on Hour of Power, into the abyss.

Well, the translator dude says to Jody, Do you come here of your own free will? And Jody's all, I do. Then the guy says, You will lose a lot of blood. Perhaps you will even die. But if you survive this ritual, you will be on the way to a different plane of existence. The one who brings you to us, the woman formerly called Cat, she was once such a lamb. To surrender yourself to the dark, to let the undead feast upon you, is to step blindfolded off the edge of the bottomless pit. You must trust. You must believe. Darkness will love you. Darkness will enfold you. Darkness will shield you. Do you accept such a destiny? If you do not, speak now, and in the morning you will wake up in your own bed, and remember nothing. But if you say aye, you will never again know where you will wake up in the morning: in your own bed, on a bed of thorns, in a coffin, in the wormy earth. Think carefully before you answer, Jody Palmer. It may be that you will never again see daylight. Some who have a special affinity for our kind … make the passage in a single night … and wake to eternal darkness. For most … well, for some there is the true death … but they would never had made the crossing anyway … it's a talent you're born with. And for some, a slow, agonizing sickness that may or may not lead to death and the crossing into undeath. We cannot tell. There is no science of vampirology. Do you understand what we are telling you?

And Jody was all, Yes.

…

— And?

— I'm sorry, sir. I was just trying to remember the details. After this it gets kinda all confused.

— Take your time, Jeremy.

— Yessir. Thank you, sir.

— You're telling us that these … creatures … made an offer to your friend, and he accepted it. An offer that, he believed, would bring about his death and transfiguration … his metamorphosis into a creature beyond life.

— I reckon so, sir. I mean, there was nothing for him in the real world anyways. He was always kind of a throwaway kid.

— Did he give any impression of having been coerced into this choice?

— Maybe he didn't feel he had no choice.

— What did the defendant do next?

— He stepped forward. And the translator guy said, First comes the consummation of all carnal pleasure. Then comes the drawing of the blood. The first is your farewell to the flesh, you candidates for initiation into the Brotherhood of Blood; the second is your salutation of the spirit.

— So the defendant believed he was being initiated into some kind of vampiric existence?

— No, you got it all wrong. Them two girls was the initiates. Jody was the lamb, the offering, the sacrifice.

— He was willing to die for this?

— I reckon so.

— What happened next?

— It gets confusing, sir. Because the first part of the ritual, that was the "farewell to the flesh" thing, slowly shifted into the second part … the blood ritual. It started with the two girls undressing Jody, slowly, sexily … for example, Cat would undo one of his shirt buttons with her teeth, then Connie would do the next one down, while Cat was sort of sliding her tongue in and out between the buttons, teasing his chest. And they were all rubbing their titties up and down him. Now I knew that Jody really had never had no sex before, well, no more than third base anyways. But when they finally got the pants off him, he wasn't even hard. He just stood there, with a faraway look, fixing on some dark future he had always dreamed about. But the two girls were at him like there was no tomorrow. I guess, for them, in a way, there wasn't. They surrounded him. They were a blur of arms and legs and lips and tongues and gleaming pussies. I couldn't believe it, but mousy Constance was the wilder of the two bitches. She was squeezing Jody's scrawny ass, pumping against him, even thrusting her tongue in his butthole. But Cat was more playful. She skimmed her tongue along his arms, his fingers, and when she reached his balls and started flicking at them, he finally started to get aroused. I think he was holding himself in, trying to resist, thinking to himself that giving in sex was some kind of weakness, that he was there for the violence, not the sex … but no red-blooded guy could stay soft forever with them two working him over. And now they were taking turns, one holding him upright while the other slid up and down on him, spinning him around, making him dizzy, and he was moaning now, I couldn't make out all of it but it was all sick, private stuff, about his childhood, his parents, I don't know … and then it started to turn toward violence … first one girl then the other was raking at him with her nails, nails that seemed to get longer and sharper … nails that seemed to curl up, tighten, into claws … the girls were bucking and heaving as they pushed him down against the middle coffin, where the vampire master dude was still sitting, watching, his eyes slowly reddening … or was that just the flickering of the torches? … I don't know … and the crowd in black was hemming in closer … making it harder for me to see … and I knew they weren't noticing me anymore, I even felt safe creeping out from behind the statue … keeping low to the ground … peering through the sea of legs and cloaks … glimpses now … the girls licking their lips … their eyes slitting … bending over him … slicing at his chest, his abdomen with their animal claws … and biting now … I could see fangs. They all had fangs. All them black-clad people with them glowing white faces. Their fangs glistened in the dark like a thousand stars. And there were other sharp things. I saw spikes … razor blades … pocket knives … hypodermics … all ready to harvest my best friend's lifeblood. The girls were still all over him … pleasure transforming into pain … but the others were moving in now … I could see a razor slice just beneath his nipple … I could see a delicate mouth close in on his ankle … and Jody was all convulsing now, I couldn't tell if it was from like an orgasm or whether they was killing the fuck out of him. Jesus I was scared. I wanted it to stop. Me against a hundred bloodsuckers, what was I thinking? But that was my best friend out there. But did you ever see a big that's been hit on the head in the slaughterhouse? That's how it looked. I mean, he was shaking like a fucking piledriver. I couldn't stand it. I mean, Jody, you know? Friends since the sixth grade. Campouts, swimming holes, dirty websites, all the shit young guys grow up together doing. Well, what I done was dumb.

— What did you do, Mr. Kindred?

— Well, I ripped the cross of the Archangel Michael's neck, and I pulled off the sword, and like a wild man I charged.

— You attacked a crowd of … sadistic vampire cultists?

— Cultists? Hell no, sir, these people was actual vampires. Cause when the shadow of the cross fell upon them, they started screaming. And scattering. And I was screaming too, a pretty damn impressive scream for a kid, a scream like a banshee, and swinging that big old heavy sword like it was nothing more'n a letter opener. Shit, I scared the fuckers. I think. There was this big flapping noise. Dust everywhere. Swirling. Mist. Everything was whirling and there was this roar, like a tornado or something. I don't think I actually hit anything with the sword. Everything was dissolving before I could smash bronze against flesh. I saw Jody on the ground there in front of the middle coffin. He was naked and I swear to God he was half drained already. There was so much blood, just sluicing from a hundred cuts on him, pouring out onto the rocky floor. I knelt down and tried to lift him up, but he was heavy, there won't no give to him at all, it was like he was already dead. I was still all crazed and I shook him, I was all, Wake up, Jody, this is your buddy telling you, come out of it, you ain't dead yet. And then the weirdest thing of all happened. You know all that swirling mist I was talking about? Well, it seemed to gather up the coffins and the cave walls and even the swordless St. Michael over there, and even the dirt beneath us, and it was all billowing about us and darkening, and the torches were blowing out one by one, and my friend was stirring a little, and I was all, Jody, don't die, don't die, don't die, when all at once the world seemed to melt around us … like a dissolve in a movie … and we were somewhere else. I smelled a fresh wind. Flowers. Old trees and rotting leaves. We were in the hills. The cemetery was way below us … and the moon was shining through the treetops. What happened? When I arrived at the cemetery there'd been cars every where, pickups, Mustangs, a Mercedes, a police car … now I couldn't see a one in that parking lot … and the graveyard was deserted. Jody was still lying across my lap … still bleeding to death … or was he? In the bright moonlight I saw … the wounds closing up … the scratches fading … the blood sort of evaporating, melding into the night mist … I didn't understand. I knew it won't no dream. I knew it had to be real … but … Jody was moaning now. I was all, Wake up, wake up … and, slowly, he did.

— I see. *And I awoke and found me here, on the cold hill's side.*

— Yeah. I guess so.

— You saved your friend's life.

— Maybe, but he sure didn't thank me for it.

— No?

— Shit, no, sir. When he come to, it was just about twilight, and I'd been watching him, and I'd covered him with my own jacket, and I was trying my ass off to make him come back into the world … and when he finally opened his eyes, well, he didn't look like he was fixing to thank me at all. He looked at me with slitted eyes, and I saw hate. Pure, naked hate. I sure was shocked. I said, Jody, it's me, your best friend, Jer. They were gonna kill you in there. I don't know what happened, but I got you out … somehow. And he whispers to me, gasping for breath between every word, like he's struggling to keep from slipping back into darkness, Jer, I wanted it. That was my chance. I'm nobody in this world. I was about to be something. Let go of me, Jeremy, and don't come near me again. And he shook off my jacket … stood up … just as the first rays of sunlight were breaking over the gravestones below yonder … he stood up, naked as the day he was born, stood up and walked away from me. He was so frail and thin he was almost like a little kid. But here's the weird thing … the scars was all healed. There won't a scratch on that boy. The sun painted him a golden sort of color, and he didn't hardly seem human. And he walked away. Away from the coming light … into the thickest part of the wood … like he was afraid of the sun.

— Did you speak to him after that?

— Not really. I think he tried to go back to one of their cemetery parties … they usually had them on the full moon … but I know he never was able to get back inside that monument. That stone carving of the jaws of hell … well, stone was all it was to him. He had lost the key. I took it from him. I was stupid, I guess. I really didn't understand him after all. He fell in with other kids. Started a new "secret society" of some kind. A wannabe vampire society. I heard about it mostly from —

— Your Honor, this is all hearsay now.

— Sustained.

— Your Honor, we have already heard evidence about young Jody Palmer's secret society … from all sorts of expert witnesses as well as from the ex-members themselves. I'm not seeking to add anything to the record on that matter from this witness. In fact, I'm going to excuse him now. Perhaps my opponents would care to cross?

— Yes, we would. Just a couple of questions, Jeremy Kindred. You're still under oath.

— Yes, ma'am.

— Isn't it true that no one has related any of these outlandish incidents … except you? I'm not referring merely to the supernatural events you claim to have seen inside one of the town's most famous landmarks … but to these very imaginative orgies you describe as having occurred regularly at the cemetery. If these things were true, don't you think others would have reported them to the authorities?

— Hell no, ma'am. Half the authorities were in them orgies.

— So it's a kind of … ah, conspiracy? Half the town involved in dark goings-on, and covering up the mess from the other half?

— You tell me, ma'am. After all, you were there, too.

— Well!

— Your Honor, the witness has just claimed that the state's prosecutor was present at those proceedings, in the light of which —

— Oh, nonsense, counselor. The boy's a raving lunatic.

— Your Honor, comments like that would tend to throw some doubt on your own impartiality —

— Shut up, counselor! I'm running a courtroom, not a voodoo séance. If the prosecution would care to continue the cross —

— Ah … no further questions.

— The witness may stand down.

— I would like to remind the defense that this evening's extraordinary timing was designed to let us hear from whoever is supposed to be inside that coffin of yours, and that we are now ten minutes past sundown. And no one has been banging on the lid from the inside. Is that particular bit of nonsense over with?

— I don't think so, sir. At this time I would like to ask the bailiff to remove the coffin lid and invite the next witness to the stand.

— All right. Bailiff?

— There's nothing inside of here, sir, except a headless cat. And a large quantity of garlic.

— That, counsel, is in very poor taste.

— I don't know how that could have happened, Your Honor! Our resident vampirologist assured us that —

— Ew, Your Honor! It's stiff.

— Dispose of it, bailiff. So what is the meaning of this, counsel? Vampire hunters been calling, I suppose?

— I have no idea what's happened at all, Your Honor. We'll have the witness for you tomorrow, I promise.

— Don't make promises you can't keep, counselor; I'm told that the dead are notoriously inept at keeping their appointments.

— Your Honor is pleased to joke at my expense.

— My Honor has had enough for the day, and we'll reconvene tomorrow morning at … let's say ten o'clock.

❧

— Dr. Shimada, you're a vampirologist.

— Just an avocation, actually. My day job is psychiatric resident at the juvenile division of the state hospital for the criminally insane. My study of vampires, real and imagined, grew out of the ramblings of a patient I have in my private practice; I can't elucidate further without breaching confidentiality, of course.

— And you've studied the defendant at some length.

— Oh, yes. Fascinating boy. Very disturbed.

— The defendant is not, however, in your professional opinion, a vampire.

— No.

— Nor any other supernatural creature.

— Well, I would take issue with the choice of "supernatural", sir, since, as I scientist, I would prefer a rational explanation for any phenomenon, however supernatural-seeming. But no, Mr. Palmer is by no means undead. He is quite, quite human. He's just like you and me.

— Except that he hasn't talked since … the events that have brought us all here for this trial.

— That is almost true. I was starting to make some progress with that. I think he needs a few more months before he'll actually … be able to say anything to shed light upon this case.

— You were making progress?

— He grunts now, sometimes. I even detected a whimper once. And one time, on my way out, in the doorway, I heard a distinct, if sotto voce, utterance of the phrase "Fuck off."

— I see. Will he ever talk?

— Everything he wants to say is caged up inside him. It only needs … a key. I've been considering the possibility of circumventing the lengthy period of therapy and just jumping to Pentothal.

— Sodium Pentothal? The old "truth serum," that cliché of 50s B-grade detective thrillers?

— The very same.

— How many sessions did you have with the defendant?

— I've seen him twice a week since the arrest.

— In your opinion, is the defendant insane?

— I think that would be obvious even to a layman.

— Was he insane at the time of the crime?

— Clearly he was unable to distinguish right from wrong at the time of the multiple murders.

— What is the nature of the defendant's mental illness?

— In Freudian terms, his superego, the inner voice we often think of as our "conscience", weak to start off with from inadequate childhood reinforcement, has disappeared entirely. It has been replaced by what he perceives as supernatural "beings", creatures who control him. He has experienced a transference of the normal youthful libido … the sex urge … in the direction of violence and bloodshed. The weakening of the superego causes him to be unable to control his beast within, his id. That, of course, is the basic reason for all crime, but in his case the weakening of the ego is clearly at a pathological level.

— I see, Dr. Shimada. I'd like to move that Dr. Shimada's entire report … some 2,310 pages of it … be admitted to the record as Exhibit, ah …

— Defense Exhibit QQ.

— Yes. Defense Exhibit QQ.

— I hope you're not expecting our benighted jurors to make head or tail of it, counselor. Even the last few minutes have been a little, ah, dry.

— Dr. Shimada's learned testimony merely adds to that of seven other psychiatrists, Your Honor, who have all agreed that the defendant is hopelessly, irretrievably insane.

— Quite so.

— Dr. Shimada, if you state again, in simple layman's terms, the defendant's state of mind before, during, and after the crimes were committed?

— In layman's terms, Jody Palmer was stark, staring bonkers, counselor.

— No further questions.

— Cross?

— Well, yes, I do have a couple of quick questions. Dr. Shimada, in this 2,000 page document which, I admit, I haven't read, although my researchers have combed through it pretty thoroughly … do you not basically say that the defendant had no conscience?

— I suppose you could put it that way.

— Well, well, well. No conscience. And for that, we're gonna let him off after he mutilated his parents, disemboweled his sister, devoured his two-year-old brother's liver, and led a gang of hooligans on a rampage that culminated in several more people becoming … unwilling blood donors … not to mention … necrophilia.

— Your Honor, the prosecution's grandstanding.

— Sustained. Just ask the questions.

— Right. Well, I really just have one more question. You say the defendant has retreated behind a wall of silence.

— Yes. It's called hysterical mutism. It's one of the ultimate defense mechanisms of the paranoid schizophrenic.

— So you compiled a 2,000 page report about this patient … without exchanging a single bit of dialogue with him?

— As I spoke to him, I monitored his vital signs, his brain waves, the surface electrical activity of his skin.

— But he didn't actually tell you any of this.

— Scientists can read a great deal from —

— He didn't actually tell you. Answer the question, please.

— Ah … no.

— No further questions.

— Natalie McConnell, you've been given immunity because you appear not to have participated in the actual killing. But you saw everything, and your insight into the defendant's state of mind is vital to the court's understanding of his motives.

— Yes, sir.

— Are you currently enrolled in Kramer High?

— No, sir. I dropped out. I had to go to work in my dad's doughnut store.

— So you never knew the defendant until a few months before the incident.

— Yes, sir. I met him at Cat Sperling's funeral.

— You know Cat Sperling, then.

— Oh, sure, sir. Everyone did. She was the town slut.

— How did you come to be aware of that?

— My daddy always said that if I behaved anything like her, he'd whup my butt till it was bloody.

— What kind of behavior constituted "behaving like Cat Sperling"?

— Um … too much lipstick … wearing leather … standing a certain way … talking in a sexy voice …

— Your father ever carry out his threat?

— Shit yeah. He wore me out all the time. When he wasn't making me go down on him.

...

— Order in the court! Order! Order! Counselor, tell the witness to stay on the topic.

— Your Honor, the fact that the witness was one of the disenfranchised, the violated members of society ... is not entirely irrelevant to this defense ... although I did not intend to have the matter raised quite this abruptly.

— That's enough. The jury will ignore the witness's life story, and concentrate only on those facts she raises that bear on this case. Meanwhile, I'd like the bailiff to make a note of the girl's remarks and pass them on the the district attorney; we are state employees here, and there are mandatory reporting laws.

— Well, judge, if you're gonna turn in my dad, you might as well turn in the pastor of Hillside Baptist Church as well. And the Vice-Principal of Kramer High — he got me in the closet one day. Oh, and —

— Miss McConnell, enough of that. When your testimony is through, you are to report to Detective ... ah ... who's on duty out there? ... Detective Arnold. He'll take it from there. Meanwhile, if the court would care to turn its attention back to the case ... Counsel? Counsel?

— Oh. Yes, Your Honor. So, despite Cat Sperling's reputation, you went to her funeral?

— Yeah. Her dad had ordered ten dozen doughnuts, you see, for afterwards, and I stopped by to get directions to the house. And that's when I saw Jody ... the defendant. He was standing in the distance ... in the shade of an oak tree. He was all in black. Trenchcoat and all. He looked lonely. Not like he was really invited. He was staring at all the relatives, at the coffin, at everything. With a kind of longing in his eyes. The guy seemed so sad. I wanted to talk to him. So I did.

— What did you converse about?

— Well, at first, I was all, like, questions, how did she die and such. And he said, Anemia. Which wasn't what I heard, I'd heard it was from something to do with sex, AIDS or such. It didn't matter nohow, cause she was gone no matter how you looked at it. I got him to give me directions to the Sperling place, and then he got to staring at me in a way I never been stared at before. Like he could see right into my mind. And he said to me, Are you afraid of the dark? And I said, Yeah. And he said, Very afraid? And I said,

Yeah. And he said, Why? And I said, Because things come to me in the night. And he said, I can take that fear away for ever. I can take you on a journey with me. Across the river of death. To the farthest shore. To the kingdom of ultimate darkness. I look into your eyes and I see you're like me, you don't got nothing to lose. I said, You sure are right about that. He said, I'm gathering a group of people to take with me on this journey. It's a quest, you see. Like searching for the Holy Grail. The cup of blood. I just know you want to come with me, Natalie. I can see it in your eyes. One time, I met these creatures from a place beyond our world. They called out to me. But I stayed behind. I had work left to do in the world. I wanted to go, but I thought of all the dispossessed of the world, all the young ones crying out for release, and I knew I had to bring a few with me in order to be worthy of my place among the dark ones.

— Did the defendant mention Jeremy Kindred at all? The fact that his friend physically prevented him from being sucked into the vampire world?

— No.

— So you had no idea there was any side to the story other than what you were being told.

— That's right, sir.

— Did you believe him?

— Not really, sir. I thought he'd lost it. But there was something real hypnotic about his voice and such. He was sexy, too. In a scary kind of way.

— Sexy and scary?

— He was pale and thin. His cheeks were all sunken and his eyes, too. He looked like he hadn't eaten in days and he'd stayed out of the sun … well, like he was dead, really. Dead but beautiful. I guess what was exciting about him was … there was a wrongness. About the way he moved. The way he smiled. Like they weren't his lips, his limbs. Do you know what I mean? Like something was animating his body and such. Possession or something. I touched his shoulder. Flinched from it. It was cold as ice. But then again I felt I wanted to warm him up all over. I wanted to give him what I'd denied all those other men who took what they wanted from me. He was different. I wanted to make love to him. And later, we went back to the doughnut van, and, in the back, I did make love to him. I think of it as that, though he didn't really do much. I did all the moving. I'd never used dad's van for that before, and it was sticky on account of all the bits of custard filling and the little patches of spilled powdered sugar and all. He sat back against a pile of delivery boxes and I didn't care that they were getting all crushed. I just ate him up, impaled myself on him, rode him up and down, wrapped my titties around his face, but all the while he was muttering about other things … about banging and banging on the gates of hell till his fists were raw and bloodied from the rough stone … I didn't know what he meant until that night, when I met him again at the Forbin-St.Cloud monument and saw him kneeling at the carved mouth of hell and beat his fists against the granite … but I didn't care you see because I'd found someone as lost as me, maybe even more lost, someone I could give to freely, someone I could love.

— So you became a member of his … secret society.

— If you could call it that. It was just him and three of us girls. He called us the Brides of Dracula. He drank our blood. He mixed it with vanilla syrup and ice in a blender. Said he needed the ice because the heat of the blood would send him straight to the other world, and he wasn't ready yet, he still had things to do in the human world. The other two girls were Ramona and Chastity. They're dead now. He found Ramona lurking outside a homeless shelter over there in the city. Chastity was a runaway. I know what we done was wrong, but Jody, well, he had a vision and such. When he talked, we felt we belonged to something big. He gave us a structure, too, our nightly hunts. He taught us to pounce on alley cats and bite their necks and slurp down the gushing blood. That was disgusting, but it was kinda thrilling too. And now and then as a really special treat he'd fuck us. But it was always with us doing all the work, and him staring off into space, thinking I guess about his great vision. Which he finally explained to us. The day before … you know.

— He told you … what? That you were going to go on a killing spree?

— Not exactly. I remember it perfectly because we were having another meeting in dad's van. We always used it for meetings now, because I could always get the van between deliveries, and now, behind the smell of apple-cinnamon and chocolate, there was also a permanent smell of sex. Because the three of us … the girls I mean, not Jody … we'd do stuff in there while we were waiting for him. Thing is, you know how it is when us girls hang out together all the time … our periods kind of fall into sync. And so all three of us were on the rag at the same time. And we were all laughing about it, how it had gotten closer and closer in the last two months and now, this time, third time lucky and such, bang, same day, same second practically. And we were all idly fingerbanging each other while we talked about our fucked-up lives. So finally he shows up. And he's all, I smell blood. God, I smell blood! It makes me feel all … oh, I want it, I want it. And since we're all already with our panties down, and all moist from playing with each other, he's all over us, pulling out our tampons, lapping at us like a cat cleaning its ass. God, it was hot! I never felt that way before. The way he flecked my clitoris, the way he tickled my lips, teasing out every last flake of coagulating blood …

— Your Honor, spare us this pornography! Objection, objection!

— Your Honor, this evidence speaks directly to the nature of the defendant's mental illness … his delusional obsession with the, ah, sanguinary aspects of the human body.

— Young lady, get it over with, and proceed to the question at hand.

— Yes, Your Honor. Um … what were you going to ask me, sir?

— Well, Natalie. You've just explained that Jody became unusually animated as a result of the smell of blood.

— That's true, sir. As I say, usually he would just lay there while we rubbed up and down on him, but that day he was excited. He even came. I mean, he just spurted.

— I don't think we need to know all that, but did the defendant then say anything about his grand vision?

— Oh yes.

— What did he say?

— Well, as we all lay there in the back of the van, there was this good, warm feeling, you know, us against the world and such, a little tiny piece of heaven. But then Jody begins to talk about the dark path we have to trod. I had my foot in the door, he said, and I was pushing my way in, and they sent me back out into the world. They didn't think I was good enough. But I'm gonna show them. I'm the king of the vampires. No dead dude in a coffin is gonna be badder than me.

— Did this statement contradict previous statements of his to you and your group of followers?

— Yes, sir. He always told us he was sent up here from the other world, that he had given up the world beyond so he could find disciples and teach all of them the dark path before he went back. Now he sounded bitter and angry and we didn't know what to do.

— What did he say next?

— We're going to do something really big, he said. An orgasm of blood and pain. We're gonna kill, maim, disembowel, decapitate, swim in the lubricious life force that spews from the veins of the dying. The way he said it, you gotta believe, it sounded … poetic …

beautiful … I could feel the blood rushing joyfully from my pussy to meet his eager tongue … I could think about nothing but all that blood, swirling over me, carrying me toward the final climax in waves of crimson passion, oh God, Jody made me feel that good, all of us, he made us want to kill and to die the way we wanted his arms around us, his cock inside us and such.

— And how do you feel about Jody now?

— I love him, sir.

— Do you think he hears you, hiding as he does behind his wall of self-imposed silence?

— I don't know. Yeah. Maybe not. Maybe he doesn't hear any of us no more, maybe he's listening to a different music, the rushing of the river of death.

— I want to spare the jury yet another description of the crimes themselves … the slashing, the torture … all the things you witness but did not participate in … because you … had a twinge of conscience.

— I chickened out. I shoulda done them things. Like all the other girls did.

— Then you would be in trouble, Natalie.

— I don't care! Do you understand? I love him. I want to go with him! Into the ultimate kingdom. Into the dark country. Jody, listen to me, you motherfucker … I didn't mean to betray you … I'm here because I want them to know the truth … what you mean to me …

— Your Honor, the witness isn't supposed to be talking to the defendant.

— Sustained. Kindly confine your comments to the questions asked of you, Miss —

— Your Honor! The coffin! It's busting open! The lid is sliding again!

— Got a stake handy, bailiff? You can use my gavel as a mallet, you superstitious nincompoop. You people are … screw it, let whoever it is come out. If the ladies and gentlemen of the jury would refrain from panicking — and just what the hell do you think you're doing in my courtroom, young lady, in the nude? Have you no sense of propriety at all? Bailiff, fetch the witness a damn cloak.

— Jody.

— Young lady, you're not on the stand yet. Go and sit down right this minute or I'll cite you for contempt.

— Be silent!

— How dare you!

— In this human world, you may be a judge of men, Mr. Trepte, but there are darker courtrooms, and there are punishments more dire than death. I stand before you, a naked woman, whose flesh is colder than the grave. Touch me if you dare.

— Madam, there is no higher authority present in this chamber than this jury and this judge. If you have anything to say, you will have to wait your turn.

— So what do you plan to do, asshole, cite me for contempt?

— Bailiff, cuff her!

— Your Honor, she's just ripped off the bailiff's head!

Sobering isn't it, Mr. Kangaroo Court, to see your enforcing officer's torso twitching on the carpet. I'm sorry that I won't be paying the dry cleaning bill. Where I come from, we don't have money … or credit cards, for that matter.

— Uh — uh —

— Speechless, at last, Your Honor! Give me a minute while I take a sip from this poor man's gushing jugular. Excuse me while I wipe my lips clean with his matted hair. Where shall I throw it? You have a basket? Thanks. Now … where was I? Oh yes. The defendant. The silent one. You who heard voices in the night, who were labeled a paranoid schizophrenic by Doctor Shimada over there … you who have been true to your deep dark self, all this time, you who have kept the faith … I've come for you. I ain't Cat Sperling, the town slut, no more … I've worked on my accent some … you learn a lot when you hang with the undead … plenty of sixty-four dollar words in their vocabulary when they've been around a couple of centuries. Look at me, silent boy. I like that you kept silent after it was over. You betrayed no one. Oh! bullets! My, my. They go right through me. I feel nothing. No feeling, you know, when you cross over the river. No mortal feelings anyways. Look at me, silent boy. I'm still beautiful, ain't I? Beautiful as the day you saw me. My body is as firm as when you first touched it, but now it's cold as marble. It's a dead body, Jody, a corpse. But oh, a corpse that everyone in this room wants, man and woman, a corpse that exudes a sensuality that the living can't match, a corpse that breathes eternity, eternity … Oh, Jody, you don't know how long you were watched, how long you were groomed for that moment of sacrifice that your friend ruined for you. Oh, he meant well. But he's just an ignorant human being. And human beings are just cattle. They're here to serve us. Their lives are over in an instant. I watched over you … saw you grow up alienated … knew you were marked to become one of us. In this world a throwaway, one of the disenfranchised … in the world beyond … a prince. When you had your fantasies of death … when you dreamed of death and woke up with a stiffie in the night … one of us was watching … perhaps in the shape of a mist, coiling about the keyhole of your bedroom door … or a black rat, sniffing its way along the floorboards … smelling the crimson of your dreams. Oh, Jody, it was all meant for you … my seduction of your dumb, sentimental friend … the party at the cemetery … partly real, partly a fabric of hypnotizing illusions. Do you understand that? Oh, your doctor noted it all down as a dementia — delusions of grandeur — megalomania — paranoia — when it was all nothing but the truth. You heard the music of the night when others heard only wind, rain, the rustling of leaves, frightened children murmuring in their sleep. Oh, we were disappointed when you didn't die the slow death that night! You have always been special to the dark ones. All your life you've heard that whispered in your ear, you've wondered if you were going mad. Those whispers were all true. You have been anointed from birth, Jody. I wasn't kidding when I called you a prince. That's exactly what you are. The Duke couldn't welcome you into the kingdom himself. His coffin has been taken far away, for safekeeping. It's getting dangerous for us here, with all these movies and role-playing games. Lies, but flirting with the truth. He's sent me to fetch you, Jody. I told you we were all sad when you didn't come to us. Some of us wanted to fetch you by force. But the Duke said, in his wisdom, Leave him be. The darkness is strong in him. If he cannot find the true kingdom right away, he will strive to build his own kingdom … he will mirror our world in his own world … and he will make himself worthy … and when he is ready … we will bring him in. That's what I'm here for. To finish what we started. Look at me now. Look at me, translucent as alabaster, pale as moonlight; come to me. That's right. You don't need that ugly orange prison suit anymore. Those cuffs are useless now. Come to me. I twist them off with a flick of my wrist. The undead have great strength. They draw their strength from the womb of mother earth herself. Oh, Jody, come, come. Unzip that uniform and stand before me naked. Touch me. Look at the horrified faces of the judge and jury. They are so unimportant now. Slide your finger against the bailiff's blood, congealing on my breasts. Lick them. Lick the blood from the areola. Slow now, slow. I kiss you now. My teeth meet soft flesh. I taste blood. Give me your blood. Warm my stone heart with your last life-force. Oh, Jody, Jody, you are beautiful. Give me all of you. I bite your chest … your abdomen … my fangs tease at the sensitive tip of your penis … blood engorges it … blood stiffens it … blood that will soon run gushing down my throat … oh, Jody, Jody, this is the end for you, the end and the beginning … drink me now … as I drink you … the cold of death is absolute … the warmth of life is but a shadow … and now … come … come into my coffin … I don't want to sleep alone anymore … come into the coffin … into the womb … into the tomb … oh, Jody, this is love … this is death.

The transcript ends here. At least, the decipherable portion of the transcript. What follows on the tape is chaos. Screaming. Here and there a single word: blood, shit, fuck, no, no, no.

There was also the fire. The courthouse razed to the ground, the judge, the superlawyers, many others hospitalized for third-degree burns. There was also the complete disappearance of the defendant. Not a charred husk of him … not a bone … not a tooth.

There was also the silence. Not a word in the press. Not a picture in the paper. Not a clip in the news.

But you know all that. You follow the media.

Perhaps you even know about the transcript, which has been pronounced a hoax by almost every expert who has been given the privilege of examining it.

Does it matter? As a certain Roman procurator once said to a certain rabbi, in a courtroom not unlike this courtroom, two thousand years ago … What is truth?

It really doesn't matter to most of you. So stop reading now. Close the book. There's nothing to be gained from idle speculation about the nature of light and darkness … about the relationship between love and death … between desire and self-destruction. Get on with your lives. Go on. Do it.

Unless, of course, you can hear the music of the night.…

The Bird Catcher ❧

There was this other boy in the internment camp. His name was Jim. After the war, he made something of a name for himself. He wrote books, even a memoir of the camp that got turned into a Spielberg movie. It didn't turn out that gloriously for me.

My grandson will never know what it's like to be consumed with hunger, hunger that is heartache. Hunger that can propel you past insanity. But I know. I've been there. So has that boy Jim; that's why I really don't envy him his Spielberg movie.

After the war, my mother and I were stranded in China for a few more years. She was penniless, a lady journalist in a time when lady journalists only covered church bazaars, a single mother at a time when "bastard" was more than a bad word.

You might think that at least we had each other, but my mother and I never intersected. Not as mother and son, not even as Americans awash in great events and oceans of Asian faces. We were both loners. We were both vulnerable.

That's how I became the boogieman's friend.

He's long dead now, but they keep him, you know, in the Museum of Horrors. Once in a generation, I visit him. Yesterday, I took my grandson Corey. Just as I took his father before him.

The destination stays the same, but the road changes every generation. The first time I had gone by boat, along the quiet back canals of the old city. Now there was an expressway. The toll was forty baht - a dollar - a month's salary that would have been, back in the 50s, in old Siam.

My son's in love with Bangkok, the insane skyline, the high tech blending with the low tech, the skyscraper shaped like a giant robot, the palatial shopping malls, the kinky sex bars, the bootleg software arcades, the whole tossed salad. And he doesn't mind the heat. He's a big-time entrepreneur here, owns a taco chain.

I live in Manhattan. It's quieter.

I can be anonymous. I can be alone. I can nurse my hunger in secret.

Christmases, though, I go to Bangkok; this Christmas, my grandson's eleventh birthday, I told my son it was time. He nodded and told me to take the chauffeur for the day.

So, to get to the place, you zigzag through the world's raunchiest traffic, then you fly along this madcap figure-eight expressway, cross the river where stone demons stand guard on the parapets of the Temple of Dawn, and then you're suddenly in this sleazy alley. Vendors hawk bowls of soup and pickled guavas. The directions are on a handwritten placard attached to a street sign with duct tape.

It's the Police Museum, upstairs from the local morgue. One wall is covered with photographs of corpses. That's not part of the museum; it's a public service display for people with missing family members to check if any of them have turned up dead. Corey didn't pay attention to the photographs; he was busy with Pokémon.

Upstairs, the feeling changed. The stairs creaked. The upstairs room was garishly lit. Glass cases along the walls were filled with medical oddities, two-headed babies and the like, each one in a jar of formaldehyde, each one meticulously labeled in Thai and English. The labels weren't printed, mind you. Handwritten. There was definitely a middle school show-and-tell feel about the exhibits. No air conditioning. And no more breeze from the river like in the old days; skyscrapers had stifled the city's breath.

There was a uniform, sick-yellow tinge to all the displays ... the neutral cream paint was edged with yellow ... the deformed livers, misshappen brains, tumorous embryos all floating in a dull yellow fluid ... the heaps of dry bones an orange-yellow, the rows of skulls yellowing in the cracks ... and then there were the young novices, shaven-headed little boys in yellow robes, staring in a heat-induced stupor as their mentor droned on about the transience of all existence, the quintessence of Buddhist philosophy.

And then there was Si Ui.

He had his own glass cabinet, like a phone booth, in the middle of the room. Naked. Desiccated. A mummy. Skinny. Mud-colored, from the embalming process, I think. A sign (handwritten, of course) explained who he was. See Ui. Devourer of children's livers in the 1950s. My grandson reads Thai more fluently than I do. He sounded out the name right away.

Si Sui Sae Ung.

"It's the boogieman, isn't it?" Corey said. But he showed little more than a passing interest. It was the year Pokémon Gold and Silver came out. So many new monsters to catch, so many names to learn.

"He hated cages," I said.

"Got him!" Corey squealed. Then, not looking up at the dead man, "I know who he was. They did a documentary on him. Can we go now?"

"Didn't your maid tell you stories at night? To frighten you? 'Be a good boy, or Si Ui will eat your liver?'"

"Gimme a break, grandpa. I'm too old for that shit." He paused. Still wouldn't look up at him. There were other glass booths in the room, other mummified criminals: a serial rapist down the way. But Si Ui was the star of the show. "Okay," Corey said, "she did try to scare me once. Well, I was like five, okay? Si Ui. You watch out, he'll eat your liver, be a good boy now. Sure, I heard that before. Well, he's not gonna eat my liver now, is he? I mean, that's probably not even him; it's probably like wax or something."

He smiled at me. The dead man did not.

"I knew him," I said. "He was my friend."

"I get it!" Corey said, back to his Gameboy. "You're like me in this Pokémon game. You caught a monster once. And tamed him. You caught the most famous monster in Thailand."

"And tamed him?" I shook my head. "No, not tamed."

"Can we go to McDonald's now?"

"You're hungry."

"I could eat the world!"

"After I tell you the whole story."

"You're gonna talk about the Chinese camp again, grandpa? And that kid Jim, and the Spielberg movie?"

"No, Corey, this is something I've never told you about before. But I'm telling you so when I'm gone, you'll know to tell your son. And your grandson."

"Okay, grandpa."

And finally, tearing himself away from the video game, he willed himself to look.

The dead man had no eyes; he could not stare back.

He hated cages. But his whole life was a long imprisonment . without a cage, he did not even exist.

Listen, Corey. I'll tell you how I met the boogieman.

Imagine I'm eleven years old, same as you are now, running wild on a leaky ship crammed with coolies. They're packed into the lower deck. We can't afford the upper deck, but when they saw we were white, they waved us on up without checking our tickets. It looks more interesting down there. And the food's got to be better. I can smell a Chinese breakfast. That oily fried bread, so crunchy on the outside, drpping with pig fat ... yeah.

It's hot. It's boring. Mom's on the prowl. A job or a husband, whichever comes first. Everyone's fleeing the communists. We're some of the last white people to get out of China.

Someone's got a portable charcoal stove on the lower deck, and there's a toothless old woman cooking congee, fanning the stove. A whiff of opium in the air blends with the rich gingery broth. Everyone down there's clustered around the food. Except this one man. Harmless-looking. Before the Japs came, we had a gardener who looked like that. Shirtless, thin, by the railing. Stiller than a statue. And a bird on the railing. Also unmoving. The other coolies are ridiculing him, making fun of his Hakka accent, calling him simpleton.

I watch him.

"Look at the idiot," the toothless woman says. "Hasn't said a word since we left Swatow."

The man has his arms stretched out, his hands cupped. Frozen. Concentrated. I suddenly realize I've snuck down the steps myself, pushed my through all the Chinese around the cooking pot, and I'm halfway there. Mesmerized. The man is stalking the bird, the boy stalking the man. I try not to breathe as I creep up.

He pounces. Wrings the bird's neck . in one swift liquid movement, a twist of the wrist, and he's already plucking the feathers with the other hand, ignoring the death-spasms. And I'm real close now. I can smell him. Mud and sweat. Behind him, the open sea. On the deck, the feathers, a bloody snowfall.

He bites off the head and I hear the skull crunch.

I scream. He whirls. I try to cover it up with a childish giggle.

He speaks in a monotone. Slowly. Sounding out each syllable, but he seems to have picked up a little pidgin. "Little white boy. You go upstairs. No belong here."

"I go where I want. They don't care."

He offers me a raw wing.

"Boy hungry?"

"Man hungry?"

I fish in my pocket, find half a liverwurst sandwich. I hold it out to him. He shakes his head. We both laugh a little. We've both known this hunger that consumes you; the agony of China is in our bones.

I say, "Me and Mom are going to Siam. On accout of my dad getting killed by the Japs and we can't live in Shanghai anymore. We were in a camp and everything." He stares blankly and so I bark in Japanese, like the guards used to. And he goes crazy.

He mutters to himself in Hakka which I don't understand that well, but it's something like, "Don't look 'em in the eye. They chop off your head. You stare at the ground, they leave you alone." He is chewing away at raw bird flesh the whole time. He adds in English, "Si Ui no like Japan man."

"Makes two of us," I say.

I've seen too much. Before the internment camp, there was Nanking. Mom was gonna do an article about the atrocities. I saw them. You think a two-year-old doesn't see anything? She carried me on her back the whole time, papoose-style.

When you've seen a river clogged with corpses, when you've looked at piles of human heads, and human livers roasting on spits, and women raped and set on fire, well, Santa and the Tooth Fairy just don't cut it. I pretended about the Tooth Fairy, though, for a long time. Because, in the camp, the ladies would pool their resources to bribe Mr. Tooth Fairy Sakamoto for a little piece of fish.

"I'm Nicholas," I say.

"Si Ui." I don't know if it's his name or something in Hakka.

I hear my mother calling from the upper deck. I turn from the strange man, the raw bird's blood trailing from his lips. "Gotta go." I turn to him, pointing at my chest, and I say, "Nicholas."

Even the upper deck is cramped. It's hotter than Shanghai, hotter even than the internment camp. We share a cabin with two Catholic priests who let us hide out there after suspecting we didn't have tickets.

Night doesn't get any cooler, and the priests snore. I'm down to a pair of shorts and I still can't sleep. So I slip away. It's easy. Nobody cares. Millions of people have been dying and I'm just some skinny kid on the wrong side of the ocean. Me and my mom have been adrift for as long as I can remember.

The ship groans and clanks. I take the steep metal stairwell down to the coolies' level. I'm wondering about the birdcatcher. Down below, the smells are a lot more comforting. The smell of sweat and soy-stained clothing masks the odor of the sea. The charcoal stove is still burning. The old woman is simmering some stew. Maybe something magical . a bit of snake's blood to revive someone's limp dick . crushed tiger bones, powdered rhinoceros horn, to heal pretty much anything. People are starving, but you can still get those kind of ingredients. I'm eleven, and I already know too much.

They are sleeping every which way, but it's easy for me to step over them even in the dark. The camp was even more crowded than this, and a misstep could get you hurt. There's a little bit of light from the little clay stove.

I don't know what I'm looking for. Just to be alone, I guess. I can be more alone in a crowd of Chinese than up there. Mom says things will be better in Siam. I don't know.

I've threaded my way past all of them. And I'm leaning against the railing. There isn't much moonlight. It's probably past midnight but the metal is still hot. There's a warm wind, though, and it dries away my sweat. China's too far away to see, and I can't even imagine Boston anymore.

He pounces.

Leather hands rasp my shoulders. Strong hands. Not big, but I can't squirm out of their grip. The hands twirl me around and I'm looking inti Si Ui's eyes. The moonlight is in them. I'm scared. I don't know why, really, all I'd have to do is scream and they'll pull him off me. But I can't get the scream out.

I look into his eyes and I see fire. A burning village. Maybe it's just the opium haze that clings to this deck, making me feel all weird inside, seeing things. And the sounds. I think it must be the whispering of the sea, but it's not, it's voices. Hungry, you little chink? And those leering, bucktoothed faces. Like comic book Japs. Barking. The fire blazes. And then, abruptly, it dissolves. And there's a kid standing in the smoky ruins. Me. And I'm holding out a liverwurst sandwich. Am I really than skinny, that pathetic? But the vision fades. And Si Ui's eyes become empty. Soulless.

"Si Ui catch anything," he says. "See, catch bird, catch boy. All same." And smiles, a curiously captivating smile.

"As long as you don't eat me," I say.

"Si Ui never eat Nicholas," he says. "Nicholas friend."

Friend? In the burning wasteland of China, an angel holding out a liverwurst sandwich? It makes me smile. And suddenly angry. The anger hits me so suddenly I don't even have time to figure out what it is. It's the war, the maggots in the millet, the commandant kicking me across the yard, but more than that it's my mom, clinging to her journalist fantasies while I dug for earthworms, letting my dad walk out to his death. I'm crying and the birdcatcher is stroking my cheek, saying, "You no cry now. Soon go back America. No one cry there." And it's the first time some has touched me with some kind of tenderness in, in, in, I dunno, since before the invasion. Because mom doesn't hug, she kind of encircles, and her arms are like the bars of a cage.

So, I'm thinking this will be my last glimpse of Si Ui. It's in the harbor at Klong Toei. You know, where Anna landed in *The King and I.* And where Joseph Conrad anchored in *Youth.*

So all these coolies, and all these trapped Americans and Europeans, they're all stampeding down the gangplank, with cargo being hoisted, workmen trundling, fleets of those bicycle pedicabs called samlors, itinerant merchants with bales of silk and fruits that seem to have hair or claws, and then there's the smell that socks you in the face, gasoline and jasmine and decay and incense. Pungent salt squid drying on racks. The ever-present fish sauce, blending with the odor of fresh papaya and pineapple and coconut and human sweat.

And my mother's off and running, with me barely keeping up, chasing after some waxed-mustache British doctor guy with one of those accents you think's a joke until you realize that's really how they talk.

So I'm just carried along by the mob.

"You buy bird, little boy?" I look up. It's a wall of sparrows, each one in a cramped wooden cage. Rows and rows of cages, stacked up from the concrete high as a man, more cages hanging from wires, stuffed into the branch-crooks of a mango tree. I see others buying the birds for a few coins, releasing them into the air.

"Why are they doing that?"

"Good for your karma. Buy bird, set bird free, shorten your suffering in your next life."

"Swell," I say.

Further off, the vendor's boy is catching them, coaxing them back into cages. That's got to be wrong, I'm thinking as the boy comes back with ten little cages hanging on each arm. The birds haven't gotten far. They can barely fly. Answering my unspoken thought, the bird seller says, "Oh, we clip wings. Must make living too, you know."

That's when a hear a sound like the thunder of a thousand wings. I think I must be dreaming. I look up. The crowd has parted. And there's a skinny little shirtless man standing in the clearing, his arms spread wide like a Jesus statue, only you can barely see a square inch of him because he's all covered in sparrows. They're perched all over his arms like they're telegraph wires or something, and squatting on his head, and clinging to his baggy homespun shorts with their claws. And the birds are all chattering at once, drowning out the cacophony of the mob.

Si Ui looks at me. And in his eyes I see ... bars. Bars of light, maybe. Prison bars. The man's trying to tell me something. I'm trapped.

The crowd that parted all of sudden comes together and he's gone. I wonder if I'm the only one who saw. I wonder if it's just another aftereffect of the opium that clogged the walkways on the ship.

But it's too late to wonder; my mom has found me, she's got me by the arm and she's yanking me back into the stream of people. And in the next few weeks I don't think about Si Ui at all. Until he shows up, just like that, in a village called Thapsakae.

After the museum, I took Corey to Baskin-Robbins and popped into Starbucks next door for a frappuccino. Visiting the boogieman is a draining thing. I wanted to let him down easy. But Corey didn't want to let go right away.

"Can we take a boatride or something?" he said. "You know I never get to come to this part of town." It's true. The traffic in Bangkok is so bad that they sell little car toilets so you can go while you're stuck at a red light for an hour. This side of town, Thonburi, the old capital, is a lot more like the past. But no one bothers to come. The traffic, they say, always the traffic.

We left the car by a local pier, hailed a river taxi, just told him to go, anywhere, told him we wanted to ride around. Overpaid him. It served me right for being me, an old white guy in baggy slacks, with a facing-backwards-Yankees-hat-toting blond kid in tow.

When you leave the river behind, there's a network of canals, called klongs, that used to be the arteries and capillaries of the old city. In Bangkok proper, they've all been filled in. But not here. The further from the main waterway we floated, the further back in time. Now the klongs were fragrant with jasmine, with stilted houses rearing up behind thickets of banana and bamboo. And I was remembering more.

Rain jars by the landing docks . lizards basking in the sun . young boys leaping into the water.

"The water was a lot clearer," I told my grandson. "And the swimmers weren't wearing those little trunks ... they were naked." Recently, fearing to offend the sensibilities of tourists, the Thai government made a fuss about little boys skinnydipping along the tourist riverboat routes. But the river is so polluted now, one wonders what difference it makes.

They were bobbing up and down around the boat. Shouting in fractured English. Wanting a lick of Corey's Baskin-Robbins. When Corey spoke to them in Thai, they swam away. Tourists who speak the language aren't tourists anymore.

"You used to do that, huh, grandpa."

"Yes," I said.

"I like the Sports Club better. The water's clean. And they make a mean chicken sandwich at the poolside bar."

I only went to the sports club once in my life. A week after we landed in Bangkok, a week of sleeping in a pew at a missionary church, a week wringing out the same clothes and ironing them over and over.

"I never thought much of the Sports Club," I said.

"Oh, grandpa, you're such a prole." One of his father's words, I thought, smiling.

"Well, I did grow up in Red China," I said.

"Yeah," he said. "So what was it like, the Sports Club?"

... a little piece of England in the midst of all this tropical stuff. The horse races. Cricket. My mother has a rendezvous with the doctor, the one she's been flirting with on the ship. They have tea and crumpets. They talk about the Bangkok Chinatown riots, and about money. I am reading a battered EC comic that I found in the reading room.

"Well, if you don't mind going native," the doctor says, "there's a clinic, down south a bit; pay wouldn't be much, and you'll have to live with the benighted buggers, but I daresay you'll cope."

"Oh, I'll go native," Mom says, "as long as I can keep writing. I'll do anything for that. I'd give you a blowjob if that's what it takes."

"Heavens," says the doctor. "More tea?"

And so, a month later, we come to a fishing village nestled in the western crook of the Gulf of Siam, and I swear it's paradise. There's a village school taught by monks, and a little clinic where Mom works, dressing wounds, jabbing penicillin into people's buttocks; I think she's working on a novel. That doctor she was flirting with got her this job because she speaks Chinese, and the village is full of Chinese immigrants, smuggled across the sea, looking for some measure of freedom.

Thapsakae . it rhymes with Tupperware ... it's always warm, but never stifling like in Bangkok ... always a breeze from the unseen sea, shaking the ripe coconuts from the trees ... a town of stilted dwellings, a tiny main street with storefront rowhouses, fields of neon green rice as far as the eye can see, lazy waterbuffalo wallowing, and always the canals running alongside the half-paved road, women beating their wet laundry with rocks in the dawn, boys diving in the noonday heat ... the second day I'm there, I meet these kids, Lek and Sombun. They're my age. I can't understand a word they're saying at first. I'm watching them, leaning against a dragon-glazed rain jar, as they shuck their school uniforms and leap in. They're laughing a lot, splashing, one time they're throwing a catfish back and forth like it's some kind of volleyball, but they're like fishes themselves, silvery brown sleek things chattering in a singsong language. And I'm alone, like I was at the camp, flinging stones into the water. Except I'm not scared like I was there. There's no time I have to be home. I can reach into just about any thicket and pluck out something good to eat: bananas, mangoes, little pink sour-apples. My shorts are all torn (I still only have one pair) and my shirt is stained with the juices of exotic fruits, and I let my hair grow as long as I want.

Today I'm thinking of the birds.

You buy a bird to free yourself from the cage of karma. You free the bird, but its wings are clipped and he's inside another cage, a cage circumscribed by the fact that he can't fly far. And the boy that catches him is in another cage, apprenticed to that vendor, unable to fly free. Cages within cages within cages. I've been in a cage before; one time in the camp they hung me up in one in the commandant's office and told me to sing.

Here, I don't feel caged at all.

The Thai kids have noticed me and they pop up from the depths right next to me, staring curiously. They're not hostile. I don't know what they're saying, but I know I'm soon going to absorb this musical language. Meanwhile, they're splashing me, daring me to dive in, and in the end I throw off these filthy clothes and I'm in the water and it's clear and warm and full of fish. And we're laughing and chasing each other. And they do know a few words of English; they've picked it up in that village school, where the monks have been ramming a weird antiquated English phrasebook down their throats.

But later, after we dry off in the sun and they try to show me how to ride a waterbuffalo, later we sneak across the gailan field and I see him again. The Birdcatcher, I mean. Gailan is a Chinese vegetable like broccoli only without the bushy part. The Chinese immigrants grow it here, They all work for this one rich Chinese man named Tae Pak, the one who had the refugees shipped to this town as cheap labor.

"You want to watch TV?" Sombun asks me.

I haven't had much of a chance to see TV. He takes me by the lead and pulls me along, with Lek behind him, giggling. Night has fallen. It happens really suddenly in the tropics, boom and it's dark. In the distance, past a wall of bamboo trees, we see glimmering lights. Tae Pak has electricity. Not that many private homes have. Mom and I use kerosene lamps at night. I've never been to his house, but I know we're going there. Villagers are zeroing in on the house now, walking surefootedly in the moonlight. The stench of night-blooming jasmine is almost choking in the compound. A little shrine to the Mother of Mercy stands by the entrance, and ahead we see what passes for a mansion here; the wooden stilts and the thatched roof with the pointed eaves, like everyone else's house, but spread out over three sides of a quadrangle, and in the center a ruined pagoda whose origin no one remembers.

The usual pigs and chickens are running around in the space under the house, but the stairway up to the veranda is packed with people, kids mostly, and they're all gazing upward. The object of their devotion is a television set, the images on it ghostly, the sound staticky and in Thai in any case . but I recognize the show . it's I Love Lucy. And I'm just staring and staring. Sombun pushes me up the steps. I barely remember to remove my sandals and step in the trough at the bottom of the steps to wash the river-mud off my feet. It's really true. I can't understand a word of it but it's still funny. The kids are laughing along with the laugh track.

Well . that's when I see Si Ui. I point at him. I try to attract his attention, but he too, sitting cross-legged on the veranda, is riveted to the screen. And when I try to whisper to Sombun that hey, I know this guy, what a weird coincidence, Sombun just whispers back, "Jek, jek," which I know is a putdown word for a Chinaman.

"I know him," I whisper. "He catches birds. And eats them. Alive." I try to attract Si Ui's attention. But he won't look at me. He's too busy staring at Lucille Ball. I'm a little bit afraid to look at him directly, scared of what his eyes might disclose, our shared and brutal past.

Lek, whose nickname just means "Tiny", shudders.

"Jek, jek," Sombun says. The laugh track kicks in.

Everything has changed now that I know he's here. On my reed mat, under the mosquito nets every night, I toss and turn, and I see things. I don't think they're dreams. I think it's like the time I looked into Si Ui's eyes and saw the fire. I see a Chinese boy running through a field of dead people. It's sort of all in black and white and he's screaming and behind him a village is burning.

At first it's the Chinese boy but somehow it's me too, and I'm running, with my bare feet squishing into dead men's bowels, running over a sea of blood and shit. And I run right into someone's arms. Hard. The comic-book Japanese villain face. A human heart, still beating, in his hand.

"Hungry, you little chink?" he says.

Little chink. Little jek.

Intestines are writhing up out of disemboweled bodies like snakes. I saw a lot of disemboweled Japs. Their officers did it in groups, quietly, stony-faced. The honorable thing to do.

I'm screaming myself awake. And then, from the veranda, maybe, I hear the tap of my mom's battered typewriter, an old

Hermes she bought in the Sunday market in Bangkok for a hundred baht.

I crawl out of bed. It's already dawn.

"Hi, Mom," I say, as I breeze past her, an old phakomah wrapped around my loins.

"Wow. It talks."

"Mom, I'm going over to Sombun's house to play."

"You're getting the hang of the place, I take it."

"Yeah."

"Pick up some food, Nicholas."

"Okay." Around here, a dollar will feed me and her three square meals. But it won't take away the other hunger.

Another lazy day of running myself ragged, gorging on papaya and coconut milk, another day in paradise.

It's time to meet the serpent, I decide.

Sombun tells me someone's been killed, and we sneak over to the police station. Si Ui is there, sitting at a desk, staring at a wall. I think he's just doing some kind of alien registration thing. He has a Thai interpreter, the same toothless woman I saw on the boat. And a policeman is writing stuff down in a ledger.

There's a woman sitting on a bench, rocking back and forth. She's talking to everyone in sight. Even me and Sombun.

Sombun whispers, "That woman Daeng. Daughter die."

Daeng mumbles, "My daughter. By the railway tracks. All she was doing was running down the street for an ice coffee. Oh, my terrible karma." She collars a passing inspector. "Help me. My daughter. Strangled, raped."

"That inspector Jed," Sombun whispered to me. "Head of the whole place."

Inspector Jed is being polite, compassionate and efficient at the same time. I like him. My mom should hang out with people like that instead of the losers who are just looking for a quick lay.

The woman continues muttering to herself. "Nit, nit, nit, nit, nit," she says. That must be the girl's name. They all have nicknames like that. Nit means "tiny", too, like Lek. "Dead, strangled," she says. "And this town is supposed to be heaven on earth. The sea, the palm trees, the sun always bright. This town has a dark heart."

Suddenly, Si Ui looks up. Stares at her. As though remembering something. Daeng is sobbing. And the policeman who's been interviewing him says, "Watch yourself, chink. Everyone smiles here. Food falls from the trees. If a little girl's murdered, they'll file it away; they won't try to find out who did it. Because this is a perfect place, and no one gets murdered. We all love each other here . you little jek."

Si Ui has this weird look in his eye. Mesmerized. My mother looks that way sometimes . when a man catches her eye and she's zeroing in for the kill. The woman's mumbling that she's going to go be a nun now, she has nothing left to live for.

"Watch your back, jek," says the policeman. He's trying, I realize, to help this man, who he probably thinks is some kind of village idiot type. "Someone'll murder you just for being a stupid little chink. And no one will bother to find out who did it."

"Si Ui hungry," says Si Ui.

I realize that I speak his language, and my friends do not.

"Si Ui!" I call out to him.

He freezes in his tracks, and slowly turns, and I look into his eyes for the second time, and I know that it was no illusion before.

Somehow we've seen through each other's eyes.

I am misfit kid in a picture-perfect town with a dark heart, but I understand what he's saying, because though I look all different I come from where he comes from. I've experienced what it's like to be Chinese. You can torture them and kill them by millions, like the Japs did, and still they endure. They just shake it off. They've outlasted everyone so far. And will till the end of time. Right now in Siam they're the coolies and the laborers, and soon they're going to end up owning the whole country. They endure. I saw their severed heads piled up like battlements, and the river choked with their corpses, and they outlasted it all.

These Thai kids will never understand.

"See Ui hungry!' the man cries.

That afternoon, I slip away from my friends at the river, and I go to the gailan field where I know he works. He never acknowledges my presence, but later, he strides further and further from the house of his rich patron, towards a more densely wooded area past the fields. It's all banana trees, the little bananas that have seeds in them, you chew the whole banana and spit out the seeds, rat-tat-tat, like a machine gun. There's bamboo, too, and the jasmine bushes that grow wild, and mango trees. Si Ui doesn't talk to me, doesn't look back, but somehow I know I'm supposed to follow him.

And I do.

Through the thicket, into a private clearing, the ground overgrown with weeds, the whole thing surrounded by vegetation, and in the middle of it a tumbledown house, the thatch unpatched in places, the stilts decaying and carved with old graffiti. The steps are lined with wooden cages. There's birdshit all over the decking, over the wooden railings, even around the foot trough. Birds are chattering from the cages, from the air around us. The sun has been searing and sweat is running down my face, my chest, soaking my phakhomah.

We don't go up into the house. Instead, Si Ui leads me past it, toward a clump of rubber trees. He doesn't talk, just keeps beckoning me, the curious way they have of beckoning, palm pointing toward the ground.

I feel dizzy. He's standing there. Swaying a little. Then he makes a little clucking, chattering sound, barely opening his lips. The birds are gathering. He seems to know their language. They're answering him. The chirping around us grows to a screeching cacophony. Above, they're circling. They're blocking out the sun and it's suddenly chilly. I'm scared now. But I don't dare say anything. In the camp, if you said anything, they always hurt you. Si Ui keeps beckoning me: nearer, come nearer. And I creep up. The birds are shrieking. And now they're swooping down, landing, gathering at Si Ui's feet, their heads moving to and fro in a regular rhythm, like they're listening to . a heartbeat. Si Ui's heartbeat. My own.

An image flashes into my head. A little Chinese boy hiding in a closet ... listening to footsteps ... breathing nervously.

He's poised. Like a snake, coiled up, ready to pounce. And then, without warning, he drops to a crouch, pulls a bird out of the sea of birds, puts it to his lips, snaps its neck with his teeth, and the blood just spurts, all over his bare skin, over the homespun wrapped around his loins, an impossible crimson. And he smiles. And throws me the bird.

I recoil. He laughs again when I let the dead bird slip through my fingers. Pounces again and gets me another.

"Birds are easy to trap," he says to me in Chinese, "easy as children, sometimes; you just have to know their language." He rips one open, pulls out a slippery liver. "You don't like them raw, I know," he says, "but come, little brother, we'll make a fire."

He waves his hand, dismisses the birds; all at once they're gone and the air is steaming again. In the heat, we make a bonfire and grill the birds' livers over it. He has become, I guess, my friend. Because he's become all talkative. "I didn't rape her," he says.

Then he talks about fleeing through the rice fields. There's a war going on around him. I guess he's my age in his story, but in Chinese they don't use past or future, everything happens in a kind of abstract now-time. I don't understand his dialect that well, but what he says matches the waking dreams I've had tossing and turning under that mosquito net. There was a Japanese soldier. He seemed kinder than the others. They were roasting something over a fire. He was handing Si Ui a morsel. A piece of liver.

Hungry, little chink?

Hungry. I understand hungry.

Human liver.

In Asia they believe that everything that will ever happen has already happened. Is that what Si Ui is doing with me, forging a karmic chain with his own childhood, the Japanese soldier?

There's so much I want to ask him, but I can't form the thoughts, especially not in Chinese. I'm young, Corey. I'm not thinking karmic cycles. What are you trying to ask me?

"I thought Si Ui ate children's livers," said Corey. "Not some dumb old birds'."

We were still on the klong, turning back now toward civilization; on either side of us were crumbling temples, old houses with pointed eaves, each one with its little totemic spirit house by the front gate, pouring sweet incense into the air, the air itself dripping with humidity. But ahead, just beyond a turn in the klong, a series of eighty-story condos reared up over the banana trees.

"Yes, he did," I said, "and we'll get to that part, in time. Don't be impatient."

"Grandpa, Si Ui ate children's livers. Just like Dracula bit women in the neck. Well like, it's the main part of the story. How long are you gonna make me wait?"

"So you know more than you told me before. About the maid trying to scare you one time, when you were five."

"Well, yeah, grandpa, I saw the miniseries. It never mentioned you."

"I'm part of the secret history, Corey."

"Cool." He contemplated his Pokémon, but decided not to go back to monster trapping. "When we get back to the Bangkok side, can I get another caramel frappuccino at Starbucks?"

"Decaf," I said.

That evening I go back to the house and find Mom in bed with Jed, the police detective. Suddenly, I don't like Jed anymore.

She barely looks up at me; Jed is pounding away and oblivious to it all; I don't know if Mom really knows I'm there, or just a shadow flitting beyond the mosquito netting. I know why she's doing it; she'll say that it's all about getting information for this great novel she's planning to write, or research for a major magazine article, but the truth is that it's about survival; it's no different from that concentration camp.

I think she finally does realize I'm there; she mouths the words "I'm sorry" and then turns back to her work. At that moment, I hear someone tapping at the entrance, and I crawl over the squeaky floor-planks, Siamese style (children learn to move around on their knees so that their head isn't accidentally higher than someone of higher rank) to see Sombun on the step.

"Can you come out?" he says. "There's a ngaan wat."

I don't know what that is, but I don't want to stay in the house. So I throw on a shirt and go with him. I soon find out that a Ngaan Wat is a temple fair, sort of a cross between a carnival and a church bazaar and a theatrical night out.

Even from a mile or two away we hear the music, the tinkling of marimbas and the thud of drums, the wail of the Javanese oboe. By the time we get there, the air is drenched with the fragrance of pickled guava, peanut pork skewers, and green papaya tossed in fish sauce. A makeshift dance floor has been spread over the muddy ground and there are dancers with rhinestone court costumes and pagoda hats, their hands bent back at an impossible angle. There's a Chinese opera troupe like I've seen in Shanghai, glittering costumes, masks painted on the faces in garish colors, boys dressed as monkeys leaping to and fro; the Thai and the Chinese striving to outdo each other in noise and brilliance. And on a grill, being tended by a fat woman, pigeons are barbecuing, each one on a mini-spear of steel. And I'm reminded of the open fire and the sizzling of half-plucked feathers.

"You got money?" Sombun says. He thinks that all farangs are rich. I fish in my pocket and pull out a few saleungs, and we stuff ourselves with pan-fried roti swimming in sweet condensed milk.

The thick juice is dripping from our lips. This really is paradise. The music, the mingled scents, the warm wind. Then I see Si Ui. There aren't any birds nearby, not unless you count the pigeons charring on the grill. Si Ui is muttering to himself, but I understand Chinese, and he's saying, over and over again, "Si Ui hungry, Si Ui hungry." He says it in a little voice and it's almost like baby talk.

We wander over to the Chinese opera troupe. They're doing something about monkeys invading heaven and stealing the apples of the gods. All these kids are somersaulting, tumbling, cartwheeling, and climbing up onto each other's shoulders. There's a little girl, nine or ten maybe, and she's watching the show. And Si Ui is watching her. And I'm watching him.

I've seen her before, know her from that night we squatted on the veranda staring at American TV shows. Was Si Ui watching her even then? I tried to remember. Couldn't be sure. Her name's Juk.

Those Chinese cymbals, with their annoying "boing-boing-boing" sound, are clashing. A man is intoning in a weird singsong. The monkeys are leaping. Suddenly I see, in Si Ui's face, the same expression I saw on the ship. He's utterly still inside, utterly quiet, beyond feeling. The war did that to him. I know. Just like it made my Mom into a whore, and me into . I don't know . a bird without a nesting place . a lost boy.

And then I get this . irrational feeling. That the little girl is a bird, chirping to herself, hopping along the ground, not noticing the stalker.

So many people here. So much jangling, so much laughter. The town's dilapidated pagodas sparkle with reflected colors, like stone Christmas trees. Chinese opera rings in my ears, I look away, when I look back they are gone . Sombun is preoccupied now, playing with two-saleung top that he just bought. Somehow feel impelled to follow. To stalk the stalker.

I duck behind a fruit stand and then I see a golden deer. It's a toy, on four wheels, pulled along a string. I can't help following it with my eyes as it darts between hampers full of rambutans and pomelos.

The deer darts toward the cupped hands of the little girl. I see her disappear into the crowd, but then I see Si Ui's face too; you can't mistake the cold fire in his eyes.

She follows the toy. Si Ui pulls. I follow, too, not really knowing why it's so fascinating. The toy deer weaves through the ocean of feet. Bare feet of monks and novices, their saffron robes skimming the mud. Feet in rubber flipflops, in the wooden sandals the Jek call kiah. I hear a voice: Juk, Juk! And I know there's someone else looking for the girl, too. It's a weird quartet, each one in the sequence known only to the next one. I can Si Ui now, his head bobbing up and down in the throng because he's a little taller than the average Thai even though he's so skinny. He's intent. Concentrated. He seems to be on wheels himself, he glides through the crowd like the toy deer does. The woman's voice, calling for Juk, is faint and distant; she hears it, I'm sure, but she's ignoring her mother or her big sister. I only hear it because my senses are sharp now, it's like the rest of the temple fair's all out of focus now, all blurry, and there's just the four of us. I see the woman now, it must be a mother or aunt, too old for a sister, collaring a roti vendor and asking if he's seen the child. The vendor shakes his head, laughs. And suddenly we're all next to the pigeon barbecue, and if the woman was only looking in the right place she'd see the little girl, giggling as she clambers through the forest of legs, as the toy zigzags over the dirt aisles. And now the deer has been yanked right up to Si Ui's feet. And the girl crawls all the way after it, seizes it, laughs, looks solemnly up at the face of the Chinaman -

"It's him! It's the chink!" Sombun is pointing, laughing. I'd forgotten he was even with me.

Si Ui is startled. His concentration snaps. He lashes out. There's a blind rage in his eyes. Dead pigeons are flying everywhere.

"Hungry!" he screams in Chinese. "Si Ui hungry!"

He turns. There is a cloth stall nearby. Suddenly he and the girl are gone amid a flurry of billowing sarongs. And I follow.

Incense in the air, stinging my eyes. A shaman gets possessed in a side aisle, his followers hushed. A flash of red. A red sarong, embroidered with gold, a year's wages, twisting through the crowd. I follow. I see the girl's terrified eyes. I see Si Ui with the red cloth wrapped around his arms, around the girl. I see something glistening, a knife maybe. And no one sees. No one but me.

Juk! Juk!

I've lost Sombun somewhere. I don't care. I thread my way through a bevy of ramwong dancers, through men dressed as women and women dressed as men. Fireworks are going off. There's an ancient wall, the temple boundary, crumbling . and the trail of red funnels into black night . and I'm standing on the other side of the wall now, watching Si Ui ride away in a pedicab, into the night. There's moonlight on him. He's saying something; even from far off I can read his lips; he's saying it over and over: Si Ui hungry, Si Ui hungry.

So they find her by the side of the road with her internal organs missing. And I'm there too, all the boys are at dawn, peering down, daring each other to touch. It's not a rape or anything, they tell us. Nothing like the other girl. Someone has seen a cowherd near the site, and he's the one they arrest. He's an Indian, you see. If there's anyone the locals despise more than the Chinese, it's the Indians. They have a saying: if you see a snake and an Indian, kill the babu.

Later, in the market, Detective Jed is escorting the Indian to the police station, and they start pelting him with stones, and they call him a dirty Indian and a cowshit eater. They beat him up pretty badly in the jail. The country's under martial law in those days, you know. They can beat up anyone they want. Or shoot them.

But most people don't really notice, or care. After all, it is paradise. To say that it is not, aloud, risks making it true. That's why my mom will never belong to Thailand; she doesn't understand that everything there resides in what is left unsaid.

That afternoon I go back to the rubber orchard. He is standing patiently. There's a bird on a branch. Si Ui is poised. Waiting. I think he is about to pounce. But I'm too excited to wait. "The girl," I say. "The girl, she's dead, did you know?"

Si Ui whirls around in a murderous fury, and then, just as suddenly, he's smiling.

"I didn't mean to break your concentration," I say.

"Girl soft," Si Ui says. "Tender." He laughs a little. I don't see a vicious killer. All I see is loneliness and hunger.

"Did you kill her?" I say.

"Kill?" he says. "I don't know. Si Ui hungry." He beckons me closer. I'm not afraid of him. "Do like me," he says. He crouches. I crouch too. He stares at the bird. And so do I. "Make like a tree now," he says, and I say, "Yes. I'm a tree." He's behind me. He's breathing down my neck. Am I the next bird? But somehow I know he won't hurt me.

"Now!" he shrieks. Blindly, instinctively, I grab the sparrow in both hands. I can feel the quick heart grow cold as the bones crunch. Blood and birdshit squirt into my fists. It feels exciting, you know, down there, inside me. I killed it. The shock of death is amazing, joyous. I wonder if this is what grownups feel when they do things to each other in the night.

He laughs. "You and me," he says, "now we same-same."

He shows me how to lick the warm blood as it spurts. It's hotter than you think. It pulses, it quivers, the whole bird trembles as it yields up its spirit to me.

And then there's the weirdest thing. You know that hunger, the one that's gnawed at me, like a wound that won't close up, since we were dragged to that camp ... it's suddenly gone. In it's place there's a kind of nothing.

The Buddhists here say that heaven itself is a kind of nothing. That the goal of all existence is to become as nothing.

And I feel it. For all of a second or two, I feel it. "I know why you do it," I say. "I won't tell anyone, I swear."

"Si Ui knows that already."

Yes, he does. We have stood on common ground. We have shared communion flesh. Once a month, a Chinese priest used to come to the camp and celebrate mass with a hunk of maggoty man to, but he never made me feel one with anyone, let alone God.

The blood bathes my lips. The liver is succulent and bursting with juices.

Perhaps this is the first person I've ever loved.

The feeling lasts a few minutes. But then comes the hunger, swooping down on me, hunger clawed and ravenous. It will never go away, not completely.

They have called in an exorcist to pray over the railway tracks. The mother of the girl they found there has become a nun, and she stands on the gravel pathway lamenting her karma. The most recent victim has few to grieve for her. I overhear Detective Jed talking to my mother. He tells her there are two killers. The second one had her throat cut and her internal organs removed ... the first one, strangulation, all different ... he's been studying these cases, these ritual killers, in American psychiatry books. And the cowherd has an alibi for the first victim.

I'm only half-listening to Jed, who drones on and on about famous mad killers in Europe. Like the butcher of Hanover, Jack the Ripper. How their victims were always chosen in a special way. How they killed over and over, always a certain way, a ritual. How they always got careless after a while, because part of what they were doing came from a hunger, a desperate need to be found out. How after a while they might leave clues ... confide in someone ... how he thought he had one of these cases on his hands, but the authorities in Bangkok weren't buying the idea. The village of Thapsakae just wasn't grand enough to play host to a reincarnation of Jack the Ripper.

I listen to him, but I've never been to Europe, and it's all just talk to me. I'm much more interested in the exorcist, who's a Brahmin, in white robes, hair down to his feet, all nappy and filthy, a dozen flower garlands around his neck, and amulets tinkling all over him.

"The killer might confide in someone," says Jed, "someone he thinks is in no position to betray him, someone perhaps too simpleminded to understand. Remember, the killer doesn't know he's evil. In a sense, he really can't help himself. He doesn't think the way we think. To himself, he's an innocent."

The exorcist enters his trance and sways and mumbles in unknown tongues. The villagers don't believe the killer's an innocent. They want to lynch him.

Women washing clothes find a young girl's hand bobbing up and down, and her head a few yards downstream. Women are panicking in the marketplace. They're lynching Indians, Chinese, anyone alien. But not Si Ui; he's a simpleton, after all. The village idiot is immune from persecution because every village needs an idiot.

The exorcist gets quite a workout, capturing spirits into baskets and jars.

Meanwhile, Si Ui has become the trusted Jek, the one who cuts the gailan in the fields and never cheats anyone of their two-saleung bundle of Chinese broccoli.

I keep his secret. Evenings, after I'm exhausted from swimming all day with Sombun and Lek, or lazing on the back of a waterbuffalo, I go to the rubber orchard and catch birds as the sun sets. I'm almost as good as him now. Sometimes he says nothing, though he'll share with me a piece of meat, cooked or uncooked; sometimes he talks up a storm. When he talks pidgin, he sounds like he's a half-wit. When he talks Thai, it's the same way, I think. But when he goes on and on in his Hakka dialect, he's as lucid as they come. I think. Because I'm only getting it in patches.

One day he says to me, "The young ones taste the best because it's the taste of childhood. You and I, we have no childhood. Only the taste."

A bird flies onto his shoulder, head tilted, chirps a friendly song. Perhaps he will soon be dinner.

Another day, Si Ui says, "Children's livers are the sweetest, they're bursting with young life. I weep for them. They're with me always. They're my friends. Like you."

Around us, paradise is crumbling. Everyone suspects someone else. Fights are breaking out in the marketplace. One day it's the Indians, another day the chinks, the Burmese. Hatred hangs in the air like the smell of rotten mangoes.

And Si Ui is getting hungrier.

My mother is working on her book now, thinking it'll make her fortune; she waits for the mail, which gets here sometimes by train, sometimes by oxcart. She's waiting for some letter from Simon and Schuster. It never comes, but she's having a ball, in her own way. She stumbles her way through the language, commits appalling solecisms, points her feet, even touches a monk one time, a total sacrilege . but they let her get away with everything. Farangs, after all, are touched by a divine madness. You can expect nothing normal from them.

She questions every villager, pores over every clue. It never occurs to her to ask me what I know.

We glut ourselves on papaya and curried catfish.

"Nicholas," my mother tells me one evening, after she's offered me a hit of opium, her latest affectation, "this really is the Garden of Eden."

I don't tell her that I've already met the serpent.

Here's how the day of reckoning happened, Corey:

It's mid-morning and I'm wandering aimlessly. My mother has taken the train to Bangkok with detective Jed. He's decided that her untouchable farang-ness might get him an audience with some major official in the police department. I don't see my friends at the river or in the marketplace. But it's not planting season, and there's no school. So I'm playing by myself, but you can only flip so many pebbles into the river, and tease so many waterbuffaloes.

After a while I decide to go and look for Sombun. We're not close, he and I, but we're thrown together a lot; things don't seem right without him.

I go to Sombun's house; it's a shabby place, but immaculate, a row house in the more "citified" part of the village, if you can call it that. Sombun's mother is making chili paste, pounding the spices in a stone mortar. You can smell the sweet basil and the lemongrass in the air. And the betelnut, too; she's chewing on the intoxicant; her teeth are stained red-black from long use.

"Oh," she says, "the farang boy."

"Where's Sombun?"

She's doesn't know quite what to make of my Thai, which has been getting better for months. "He's not home, Little Mouse," she says. "He went to the Jek's house to buy broccoli. Do you want to eat?"

"I've eaten, thanks, auntie," I say, but for politeness' sake I'm forced to nibble on bright green sali pastry.

"He's been gone a long time," she said, as she pounded. "I wonder if the chink's going to teach him to catch birds."

"Birds?"

And I start to get this weird feeling. Because I'm the one who catches birds with the Chinaman, I'm the one who's shared his past, who understands his hunger. Not just any kid.

"Sombun told me the chink was going to show him a special trick for catching them. Something about putting yourself into a deep state of samadhi, reaching out with your mind, plucking the life-force with your mind. It sounds very spiritual, doesn't it? I always took the chink for a moron, but maybe I'm misjudging him; Sombun seems to do a much better job," she said. "I never liked it when they came to our village, but they do work hard."

Well, when I leave Sombun's house, I'm starting to get a little mad. It's jealousy, of course, childish jealousy; I see that now. But I don't want to go there and disrupt their little bird-catching session. I'm not a spoilsport. I'm just going to pace up and down by the side of the klong, doing a slow burn.

The serpent came to me! I was the only one who could see through his madness and his pain, the only one who truly knew the hunger that drove him! That's what I'm thinking. And I go back to tossing pebbles, and I tease the gibbon chained by the temple's gate, and I kick a waterbuffalo around. And, before I knew it, this twinge of jealousy has grown into a kind of rage. It's like I was one of those birds, only in a really big cage, and I'd been flying and flying and thinking I was free, and now I've banged into the prison bars for the first time. I'm so mad I could burst.

I'm playing by myself by the railway tracks when I see my mom and the detective walking out of the station. And that's the last straw. I want to hurt someone. I want to hurt my mom for shutting me out and letting strangers into her mosquito net at night. I want to punish Jed for thinking he knows everything. I want someone to notice me.

So that's when I run up to them and I say, "I'm the one! He confided in me! You said he was going to give himself away to someone and it was me, it was me!"

My mom just stares at me, but Jed becomes very quiet. "The Chinaman?" he asks me.

I say, "He told me children's livers are the sweetest. I think he's after Sombun." I don't tell him that he's only going to teach Sombun to catch birds, that he taught me too, that boys are safe from him because like the detective told us, we're not the special kind of victim he seeks out. "In his house, in the rubber orchard, you'll find everything," I say. "Bones. He makes the feet into a stew," I add, improvising now, because I've never been inside that house. "He cuts off their faces and dries them on a jerky rack. And Sombun's with him."

The truth is, I'm just making trouble. I don't believe there's dried faces in the house or human bones. I know Sombun's going to be safe, that Si Ui's only teaching him how to squeeze the life force from the birds, how to blunt the ancient hunger. Him instead of me. They're not going to find anything but dead birds.

There's a scream. I turn. I see Sombun's mother with a basket of fish, coming from the market. She's overheard me, and she cries, "The chink is killing my son!" Faster than thought, the street is full of people, screaming their anti-chink epithets and pulling out butcher knives. Jed's calling for reinforcements. Street vendors are tightening their phakhomas around their waists.

"Which way?" Jed asks, and suddenly I'm at the head of an army, racing full tilt toward the rubber orchard, along the neon green of the young rice paddies, beside the canals teeming with catfish, through thickets of banana trees, around the walls of the old temple, through the fields of gailan, and this too feeds my hunger. It's ugly.

He's a Chinaman. He's the village idiot. He's different. He's an alien. Anything is possible.

We're converging on the gailan field now. They're waving sticks. Harvesting sickles. Fishknives. They're shouting, "Kill the chink, kill the chink." Sombun's mother is shrieking and wailing, and Detective Jed has his gun out. Tae Pak, the village rich man, is vainly trying to stop the mob from trampling his broccoli. The army is unstoppable. And I'm their leader, I brought them here with my little lie. Even my mother is finally in awe.

I push through the bamboo thicket and we're standing in the clearing in the rubber orchard now. They're screaming for the Jek's blood. And I'm screaming with them.

Si Ui is nowhere to be found. They're beating on the ground now, slicing it with their scythes, smashing their clubs against the trees. Sombun's mother is hysterical. The other women have caught her mood, and they're all screaming now, because someone is holding up a sandal. Sombun's.

… a little Chinese boy hiding in a closet …

The image flashes again. I must go up into the house. I steal away, sneak up the steps, respectfully removing my sandals at the veranda, and I slip into the house.

A kerosene lamp burns. Light and shadows dance. There is a low wooden platform for a bed, a mosquito net, a woven rush mat for sleeping; off in a corner, there is a closet.

Birds everywhere. Dead birds pinned to the walls. Birds' heads piled up on plates. Blood spatters on the floorplanks. Feathers wafting. On a charcoal stove in one corner, there's a wok with some hot oil and garlic, and sizzling in that oil is a heart, too big to be the heart of a bird..

My eyes get used to the darkness. I see human bones in a pail. I see a young girl's head in a jar, the skull sawn open, half the brain gone. I see a bowl of pickled eyes.

I'm not afraid. These are familiar sights. This horror is a spectral echo of Nanking, nothing more.

"Si Ui," I whisper. "I lied to them. I know you didn't do anything to Sombun. You're one of the killers who does the same thing over and over. You don't eat boys. I know I've always been safe with you. I've always trusted you."

I hear someone crying. The whimper of a child.

"Hungry," says the voice. "Hungry."

A voice from behind the closet door….

The door opens. Si Ui is there, huddled, bone-thin, his phakomah about his loins, weeping, rocking.

Noises now. Angry voices. They're clambering up the steps. They're breaking down the wall planks. Light streams in.

"I'm sorry," I whisper. I see fire flicker in his eyes, then drain away as the mob sweeps into the room.

My grandson was hungry, too. When he said he could eat the world, he wasn't kidding. After the second decaf frappuccino, there was Italian ice in the Oriental's coffee shop, and then, riding back on the Skytrain to join the chauffeur who had conveniently parked at the Sogo mall, there was a box of Smarties. Corey's mother always told me to watch the sugar, and she had plenty of Ritalin in stock - no prescription needed here - but it was always my pleasure to defy my daughter-in-law and leave her to deal with the consequences.

Corey ran wild in the skytrain station, whooping up the staircases, yelling at old ladies. No one minded. Kids are indulged in Babylon East; little blond boys are too cute to do wrong. For some, this noisy, polluted, chaotic city is still a kind of paradise.

My day of revelations ended at my son's townhouse in Sukhumvit, where maids and nannies fussed over little Corey and undressed him and got him in his Pokémon pajamas as I drained a glass of Beaujolais. My son was rarely home; the taco chain consumed all his time. My daughter-in-law was a social butterfly; she had already gone out for the evening, all pearls and Thai silk. So it fell to me to go into my grandson's room and to kiss him goodnight and goodbye.

Corey's bedroom was little piece of America, with its Phantom Menace drapes and its Playstation. But on a high niche, an image of the Buddha looked down; a decaying garland still perfumed the air with a whiff of jasmine. The air conditioning was chilly; the Bangkok of the rich is a cold city; the more conspicuous the consumption, the lower the thermostat setting. I shivered, even as I missed Manhattan in January.

"Tell me a story, grandpa?" Corey said.

"I told you one already," I said.

"Yeah, you did," he said wistfully. "About you in the Garden of Eden, and the serpent who was really a kid-eating monster."

All true. But as the years passed I had come to see that perhaps I was the serpent. I was the one who mixed lies with the truth, and took away his innocence. He was a child, really, a hungry child. And so was I.

"Tell me what happened to him," Corey said. "Did the people lynch him?"

"No. The court ruled that he was a madman, and sentenced him to a mental home. But the military government of Field Marshall Sarit reversed the decision, and they took him away and shot him. And he didn't even kill half the kids they said he killed."

"Like the first girl, the one who was raped and strangled," Corey said, "but she didn't get eaten. Maybe that other killer's still around." So he had been paying attention after all. I know he loves me, though he rarely says so; he had suffered an old man's ramblings for one long air conditioning-free day, without complaint. I'm proud of him, can barely believe I've held on to life long enough to get to know him.

I leaned down to kiss him. He clung to me; and, as he let go, he asked me sleepily, "Do you ever feel that hungry, grandpa?"

I didn't want to answer him; so, without another word, I slipped quietly away.

That night, I wandered in my dreams through fields of the dead; the hunger raged; I killed, I swallowed children whole and spat them out; I burned down cities; I stood aflame in my self-made inferno, howling with elemental grief; and in the morning, without leaving a note, I took a taxi to the airport and flew back to New York.

To face the hunger.

Beloved Disciple ❧

First off, I never fucked him.

I know, I know, Your Holiness, Your Eminences, Monsignor, distinguished fathers of the Roman and other churches; some of you are going to be disappointed. I've heard that there's even a church named in my honor, the Church of the Beloved Disciple, with the implication that I'm the patron saint of homosexuals, which is all very flattering, especially knowing how many of you reverend fathers suffer from certain ... proclivities which you hypocritically practice even though they are forbidden in your religion.

Not that it never occurred to me. For in any other country in the Empire or beyond, it would have been perfectly natural. But this was Judaea, and Joshua barJoseph, Jesus to his Greek friends, was very, very Jewish: no pork, no graven images, and no buggery.

He was so pure that I don't think he ever even masturbated. But he had a passionate hankering for all those things that make a man immortal: philosophies, ideas, poetry. And a hankering for me, too, since I was what, at the time, he was not: I was, so to speak, the real thing.

I am immortal. I am a vampire.

He was a dreamy boy — no more than a boy when I first met him, though old enough to turn a few heads in Cornwall — for the Celts, when it comes to boys, were more Greek than the Greeks, as you would know if you read Caesar's Gallic War unexpurgated.

Cornwall, you protest! Jesus was never in Cornwall. Oh, but you surely know William Blake's poem:

And did those feet in ancient time
Walk upon England's mountains green?

As late as the nineteenth century there still lingered some memory of the truth: that Joseph of Arimathea, one of the most influential men in Judaea, owned shares in a Cornish tin-mine, and had become rich from the manufacture of bronze; that he once had occasion to bring young Joshua to distant Britannia, the most barbaric outpost of the Empire.

Joshua's father was another Joseph, a rabbi of the Essene sect, so learned and so diligent that they nicknamed him The Carpenter. His mother, Miriam, doted on his little brother James, and ignored him. They were, in modern parlance, dysfunctional.

I learned all these things when I was in Cornwall for the winter solstice.

The solstice was a marvelous thing. You cannot imagine what you have lost by turning your backs on the paganism you so shamelessly plundered for the trappings of your own religion. You still burn the yule log. But the Celts burned living things: virgins, children of particular purity and beauty, lambs, chickens, cattle, all imprisoned within monstrous wicker statues, so tall they dwarfed the trees, the houses, even the menhirs or votive monoliths that the Celts loved to erect in honor of Bridget, their great goddess.

This was, you understand, before the rampant Romanization of the area. I visited it less than a century later and found a health spa, a marble shopping mall and slave market, next to a temple to the God Vespasian. The Old Religion had become unfashionable. I see you're smiling, Your Holiness; the same thing seems to have happened to your own Old Religion.

But not to digress, the solstice was a wonderful time for hunting humans, and on the night of the great sacrifices I was mingling with them, sniffing the night air, redolent with the fragrance of excited blood. Bloodlust was blowing in the wind. Druids strode among the populace, and so did I, in the same white robes, a wolf in wolf's clothing.

The feet of the wicker men were already aflame. They held the lowlier life forms; the humans, lashed together inside the statue's chest and head, would have ample time to reflect on their mortality. Most seemed resigned, though a few screamed and tried to free themselves, much to the merriment of all. I moved through the throng. There was snow on the ground, but the heat from the wicker men was turning it to mush. Boars were roasting on spits, and tourists were being fleeced by cunning vendors into buying any number of sacred stones, elixirs, mistletoe love charms, and the like. Among those tourists was a small group of Judaeans; and one, apart from the others, was gazing intently at the holocaust, almost as though he were feeling the victims' suffering with them. This was the boy called Joshua barJoseph.

I could single out the peculiar scent of his blood, even in this chaos. It was a sweet blood. In today's all-too-scientific parlance, you might say that I detected a complete absence of adrenaline; his was a terrifying kind of inner calm, almost as though he were already one of us. It was this calm I found most beautiful about him. I wanted to make him kindred to me. I did not want to feed on him, and then abandon him to the worms and fishes.

I do not breathe, and so it was I was able to stand behind him, quite close to him, without his noticing. I wanted to hold off the moment of attack, to savor the fragrance of his blood, as a mortal lover longs to delay his climax till he can bear no longer.

At last I could no longer rein myself in. The sacrificial victims were on fire. Smoke billowed through the crowd. Blood, I thought to myself; blood, blood. I coiled, prepared to pounce.

"Don't," the boy said.

It suddenly occurred to me that he had known I was there all along; perhaps he had even been toying with me.

"I have a sense about these things," he said, and turned to me. Looked me over with his soulful, serious eyes. "Joshua," he said. "And you ... I suppose you have many names. I'll call you John."

"All right."

"You're not a druid at all, are you?"

"What am I?"

"I'm not sure, really. I think you're sort of an angel."

"Hardly. I'm what you might call a fisher of men. You often talk to angels?"

"My whole family does. They're always at the house. An angel told my mother she was going to get pregnant with me, you know. Other people laughed when she said it was an angel; they said it was a Roman centurion named Pantera. Another angel told my father he should marry my mother anyway, but he still doesn't like me."

"You're here without them."

"Yes, I made a scene at my own bar mitzvah, got into a big argument with some learned men, so they sent me away with Uncle Joseph to cool off. Wasn't a scene, really. All I said was that the whole of the Torah could be boiled down to a single sentence — 'Do unto others what you would have them do unto you.' Rabbi Hillel says that all the time. I was just quoting him. They don't call him a dangerous radical."

"I'm assuming this Rabbi Hillel is a learned, venerable scholar rather than an insolent pipsqueak like yourself."

"I keep trying to go about my father's business, but I never seem to get it right."

"So they don't think you should be a rabbi."

"That's right. They want me to get into bronze, like Uncle Joseph." The Roman occupation had made Joseph of Arimathea a very rich man.

We did not talk for a while. The wicker men were fast being consumed, and the Celts were rolling around drunk and indulging in the usual debaucheries. The druids were droning an interminable paean to the sexual forces in nature, and I needed to slake my thirst. A suitable prospect ambled by at just that moment. I entranced her with a look, sipped a little from the nape of her neck even as she stared into empty space, seduced by my eyes, which seem to mortals like a yawning void. Joshua watched me, alarmed and fascinated. "You're a strange kind of angel," he said at last, as I let the woman go and she stumbled into the crowd. "You're beautiful, and that in itself is dangerous. The way your skin sucks in the moonlight. It's probably really cold, as cold as the moon."

"Yes." If only he knew how cold. I have stood in the country of the midnight sun. But what I am is a thing more desolate still. "Tell me about that sense of yours," I said. "Most people are completely clueless about what's lurking in their very midst."

"Well," Joshua said, "I just make myself go very still, and then it's like I'm outside myself."

"Samadhi," I said.

He started. "What language is that?" Almost as if he had heard it before.

"A language of India. It's something ascetics know how to do... leaving their own bodies, turning themselves into creatures of pure spirit, floating above the world. Only they have to meditate for years first."

"Oh!" he said. "You've been to India!"

"Occasionally," I said. I did not tell him how long ago.

"So have I," said the boy. And he told me all about it. I'm not sure how much there was to it. It was all so mythic: the massacre of the innocents, a flight by camel across a great desert, then forests, palaces, sages, teeming cities; and him so young through all of it, he could not possibly have remembered so much. I think he was told some of it, surmised some, imagined most of it. He had the gift that all great leaders have; he could take the wildest fancies and make them palpable.

Before long, I was telling him some of my own adventures in India. Encounters with hermits in the jungle. How I once sipped the blood of a maharani as she rode to a tryst with a secret lover on the back of an elephant. How I had sat at the feet of the Buddha and heard him tell me that the world is only a dream. He came alive as we talked. I was almost convinced he had been there.

"You see," he said, "we do have something in common."

"More that something." For he had seen the void, and he had not been afraid.

From that moment on, I wanted to make him my beloved disciple, to teach him the ways of love and death, to be his guide through the labyrinth of night. But he had other ideas. "One day," he said, "they'll hold this festival in my name. But I think I'll get rid of the human sacrificing." Even then, Your Holiness, he was suffering from what has come to be known as a messiah complex.

A bearded man, richly attired in the Hellenistic fashion, his head covering the only indication of his Judaean origins, called out to Joshua: "Let's go back now, Joshua. This place reeks of pork."

Joshua surprised me by putting his arms around me, and his lips to my lips, also in the Hellenistic fashion; I held him a little longer than was seemly, but only because I wanted to savor the pure still fragrance of his blood; perhaps, though, he mistook my meaning, for he then said, "I'd love to, but you see, I'm Jewish; we're not allowed to."

He stepped away from me, a slender, shadowy figure that soon blended into the crowd. A hint of that strange fragrance hung in the air, for the fires had died down and the celebrants mostly passed out from too much partying. I wandered among them for a while, feeding here and there. But their lust-drenched blood was too rich, too ripe.

He's only a minnow, I told myself. I've tossed him back in the river. But I couldn't shake the suspicion that it was I who had been let go. Who was fishing whom? It depressed me so much, I went to a cave in the Himalayas and slept for thirteen years.

When next I saw him, he was in his thirties. I, of course, had not aged.

"John," he said. I hate the name John. You will note that I have contrived to omit it from that gospel. But Joshua had changed. Getting dunked in the Jordan by his cousin the mad guru had caused him to undergo what you might call a religious experience. The messiah complex was in full swing, and he'd caught a bit of the infallibility bug, too, Your Holiness. Yet he was no fool. He knew me at once. Even though night was falling, and thousands of people had gathered to hear him preach.

I had braved the twilight to come and see him, cowled and caped like Mr. Death to protect myself from the dying sun. He had been preaching all day, mostly, it seems, a rehashed rendition of Rabbi Hillel's doctrines; but there was a healthy dose of Buddhism in it too, the whole non-violent "blessed are the meek" angle, half-remembered from the stories I had told him about India.

Like a guru in Benares, he was surrounded by disciples, fetching him wine, bread and fish, sitting at his feet so that not a pearl could escape.

They stared at me, with my pallid mien, my unblinking gaze, the fact that I do not breathe except occasionally, for a touch of verisimilitude. One of them, tall and bearded and reeking of fish, was about to shoo me away, but Joshua barJoseph silenced him with a barely perceptible flick of the wrist. I smelled the strange tranquility of his blood. I knew at once that this was the memory that had drawn me back from the sleep of the dead.

"Now I'm old," he said, laughing, "and you're the callow boy. You'll have to be my beloved disciple this time round." We both laughed, but the companions didn't. I made them uncomfortable. "Peter," he said to the tall one, "don't you know an angel when you see one?"

Warily, the disciples looked me over. One of them — I could tell from the family resemblance that this must be James, the favored younger brother — said, "Is he Jewish?" They were eating, you see. It wasn't as rude as you might think; dining with goyim violates one of their innumerable mitzvot.

"Don't be such a brat, James," Joshua said. "Haven't you been listening? I've changed the rules."

"You're such a fucking egotist," said James. "No one minds your being the messiah — everyone and his mother's the *kwisatz haderach* these days. But you start saying 'I've changed the rules' and people are going to think you're crazy." He wouldn't eat another bite, but the others were less fastidious.

"I'm not crazy," he said slowly. "There's got to be five thousand people camped out here tonight. They need something. I'm giving it to them. There are miracles. The blind can see. Today" — he looked straight into my eyes — "you've seen the dead walk." Peter poured me a krater of wine. "He never drinks wine," Joshua said, and made me laugh again, and baffled the others even further; grumbling, they turned away from us and began debating some arcane aspect of the Torah.

"We've got to talk," said Joshua to me. He got up suddenly from the rug they'd laid out for him. He gripped my hand. The coldness of my flesh didn't make flinch. I didn't feel his blood quicken. Only the preternatural calm. He led me a little further uphill. It was sheep country here, crags protruding out of sparse vegetation; the moon was rising now, and you could see all the followers, bundled up, dotting the slopes and on down into the valley; the sheep analogy felt particularly poignant. "I've been ... well ... waiting for you to come back," he said.

"What for?" I said.

"You're still the same. The childlike eyes. You don't need to breathe the air. You are an angel. I know I wasn't wrong when I was a boy, in Cornwall, at that awful sacrifice."

"Maybe a dark angel."

"You have to help me, John. I'm the captain of the ship, but I don't know which way to go, and I don't recognize any of the stars."

"Rabbinical teachings are hardly my thing. You haven't tried asking your father?"

"Which one?"

"Touché," I said. Inside the head of this brilliant, radical rabbi there was still the angry little boy, uncertain of his parentage, whose mother saw angels where others saw centurions.

"I've been suckered into this whole messiah scheme," he said, "but I'm all wrong for the role. I don't understand politics. I've never led an army. I don't even believe in an independent Jewish state. Have you heard of this guy Herod Agrippa? Now he'd make a fine messiah. He's had military training... and he went to school with everyone who's anyone in Rome, so he knows the enemy ... speaks Greek like a native ... plus he's got royal blood. The messiah's supposed to have royal blood."

"Genealogies can always be faked."

"Yes, but —"

"So why don't you just endorse him?"

"Yes, but... well, I know it's hopeless. The Romans are the greatest nation on earth... well, the only nation on earth. No messiah has ever succeeded before ... it's essentially a losing proposition. Unless...."

He had no intention of asking my advice at all. He was bouncing ideas off me. Well; we cast no reflection, you see. That's because we are your reflection. We hold up the mirror to your dark souls. Chew on that one, Your Holiness. I stood beside him, on the hilltop, overlooking the sea of sheep, showing him his true self in my vacant eyes.

"Unless," he went on, "the redemption of Israel is really a metaphor for something much bigger, something cosmic. Unless the kingdom is not even of this world. Do you follow me? Like the world you come from, the world of shadows. That's it, you see. If I build my church on reality, then I'm building it in the sand, and Rome is the infinite sea."

"What are you saying?"

"Nothing really. Except —"

"Except?"

"Can't you stay, this time? I know I can't turn back the clock to that time in Cornwall, and of course I'm just as Jewish as I was then, so I don't do abominations, but... you're the only one who understands. There's more to life than ... you know, life."

Had I been human my heart would have raced, my hormones would have started to hum, because Joshua was on the verge of admitting that he loved me, even though he couldn't quite bring himself to suck my dick. He still didn't quite get it, Reverend Fathers. I was going to have to use the direct approach. You never have much time, with humans. You blink and they're dead.

"I'll stay, but you're going to have to give me something," I said.

He sighed.

"No, no, you fool," I said. "I only want a little blood."

"Wouldn't be kosher," he said. "But I guess you wouldn't care about that. Well... why not? The whole world's going to be drinking my blood soon enough."

He pulled back his right sleeve and offered me his wrist. I knelt down, worried a little scab with a fingernail, then sipped it, one drop at a time. It was something to savor. That otherworldly calm seeped into me. A memory of my mortality surfaced for a moment. My mother's milk. I had not thought of mortality in a thousand years. For a moment I almost thought my heart was beating. As I drank, he stared out over the sleeping congregation. His eyes shone in the moonlight. Some humans become aroused when I feed on them, and cry out as in orgasm; he only made himself go far away.

Finally, faintly, I heard him say, half to himself, "They crucify you through the wrist; did you know that? A lot of people think it's through the palms, but that would just rip right through."

And that, Your Holiness, Your Eminences, Reverend Fathers of the Church, was the extent of the Beloved Disciples's carnal knowledge of the Son of Man.

It took some time for Joshua's followers to get used to the idea that I was there to stay. Judaea was a pretty tense place, a messiah under every rock, political activists railing in every street corner, and the Romans sitting around crucifying people almost at random. I wasn't a spy, and I wasn't one of the peasants, and I was surely no theologian. But it was necessary, for various numerological and historical reasons, to have twelve apostles, and Joshua always got his own way.

I was there for it all: the miracles, such as they were, though you people have become a lot slicker at these things; the triumphal entry into Jerusalem, carefully stage managed so as to function as an elegant midrash on selected passages of the Tanakh; I was there for the passover shabbat, wherein Joshua made no mention of his body and blood, such pagan concepts being quite distasteful to him; and I was there for the awful climax and its bathetic denouement.

After they dragged him away, the apostles called an emergency meeting at Joseph of Arimathea's house. Joshua's parents were conspicuously absent, as usual; but there was another Miriam, an ex-prostitute, who was Joshua's first and most devoted groupie and could not be kept away. Joseph — a liberal — didn't mind having harlots in the house, though he did draw the line at publicans.

"It can't end this way," James said. It was as if, having been the family's darling all his life, he couldn't stand the thought of being permanently one-upped by Joshua's martyrdom.

"So what do you suggest?" said Peter. "We can't very well storm the dungeons; we'll all end up getting strung up." He stared shiftily about; on his way to the meeting he had denied knowing Joshua three times. The foetor of his fear permeated the chamber. They were all stinking drunk, except for me.

I sat in the shadows, thinking of other things. Between mortals and immortals, love always ends in an unending longing. I wished we could have gone to India together. Or even to the world on the other side of the ocean, which I had heard about from a sage whose skin was the color of wine. I relived our first meeting again and again. Their lives rush by so fast, I thought. Larva to chrysalis to butterfly to putrefaction.

It was Joseph of Arimathea who said, "But it's so simple. Let John bring him back from the dead."

They all looked at me, looked away, drank deeply; I said, "It's a gift that can't be taken back. And he has never asked me to make him immortal."

"We need him," Peter said. "You can see that. We're like a chicken with its head cut off. If he comes back, everyone will see that the God of Abraham, Isaac and Jacob is more powerful than idols of stone and brass."

"When's the execution?" I said.

"Friday," said Joseph of Arimathea, who, being a man of influence, had a tendency to know these things. "The Romans'll give him a fair trial, but there's really no way they can let off someone who's being openly called King of the Jews."

"But his kingdom's not of this world!" said Thomas, who never believed anything he was told.

"The Romans," I said, "are completely literal-minded. That's why they own everything."

"It's politics as usual," said Joseph, "and Pilate has to protect his own ass back home. Can't blame him, really." But he was on the verge of tears. I've often wondered whether it was not he, rather than the legendary Pantera, who stuck it to the rabbi's fiancée; for he loved Joshua far more than the other Joseph ever did.

It was Joseph who convinced me, not the squabbling, self-righteous rabble who called themselves his apostles. No, I take that back, Your Holiness. It was I myself who convinced me. Perhaps it was selfishness. But you, Reverend Fathers, have never faced eternity. You just wouldn't understand.

Oh, but you preach eternity from your pulpits. Eternal bliss, eternal damnation. Fleecy clouds and fiery brimstone. You don't know what the fuck you're talking about. After the first few hundred years, every color becomes gray. Every song is a single note. Every mortal is another scurrying piece of vermin, and all that is left is the ache that can never be slaked, and the loss than festers forever. You are fools to say forever so lightly. A long long time, my friends, is not forever.

"I'll do it," I said softly. "But somehow, we have to get him to drink my blood."

"Is that kosher?" said James. No one so much as looked at him for the rest of the evening.

Humans can never get used to crucifixions, but for me an almost clinical detachment was possible. In their own way, the Romans bent over backward to accommodate the practices of their wayward subjects. Usually it takes days for the victim to die, but the Judaeans had a religious taboo against leaving corpses hanging after sunset (or was it only on Saturdays?) so they had compromised by using novel techniques for speeding up death: the flogging and the nails were, grotesquely enough, designed to shorten the agony. That was Roman knowhow for you.

The "display" crosses you see in religious paintings were not a common feature of these operations. Actually, criminals were strung up only slightly above eye level; you could look right into their faces, even spit in their eye; and people did. Public executions bring out the worst in mortals. You all know that Joshua barJoseph was crucified between two thieves, but actually the whole hillside was crammed with crosses; under Roman law, virtually everything was a capital offense.

It was afternoon, and so I almost didn't make it there. But about three or four o'clock it became preternaturally dark; a nightingale began to sing outside the room at Joseph of Arimathea's mansion where I was lying. I came to suddenly, bewildered because my sleep seemed so short. There was no one in the house. I made my way to the crucifixion hill.

In the tribal north, there had been at least a sense of elation and celebration about the wicker men. Here there was nothing of the kind. Here only beggars and lepers lurked about, and a few idle curious; the Roman soldiers, jaded, went about their business, nailing them down and stringing them up. Unrecycled crossbeams lay on the dirt; the smell of stale blood clung to them, mingled with the scent of fresh-gushing blood which permeated the hot, dry air.

I made my way through the forest of the dying, and at length spied Miriam — the whore, not the mother — standing almost at the summit of the hill, where three recent crosses formed a sort of triptych of suffering. The smell of Joshua's blood was faint, but it still held that eerie calm. I went up to Miriam, told her we had to go through with the plan.

She said, "Wait. His mother's here."

Then it was I saw another woman, one who had remained conspicuously absent throughout Joshua's ministry. She looked up at her son now, and I do not think she wept.

And I too looked, and did not weep, but for another reason; I cannot.

It was going to have to be done soon. And still I was unsure, because, Reverend Sirs, it takes more than an invitation for a man to enter my eternal kingdom — not a sprinkle of water over a baby — not a few murmured phrases. To borrow a cliché of your modern pop psychology, Joshua had to want to change. I was almost sure I had seen that longing in him, at our very first meeting... but might it have been something else?

I watched for a sign. His agony beggared description, but then all agony does, in the end, doesn't it? They had crowned him with thorns. Blood caked his forehead. There were flies. Vultures, too. The causa poenae, tacked to the cross, read "Rex Iudaeorum." He gazed back at me, his eyes already beginning to dull. In his mother's eyes I saw... disappointment, perhaps. She looked at Miriam the prostitute and for a moment I thought she was going to claw her eyes out. Then she saw me.

I do not look Jewish. I am clean-shaven as I was in life, which the Judaeans considered a sign of Hellenistic effeminacy. I have a certain clarity of complexion, a glow; all vampires do. That is why the ugliest of mortals becomes beautiful once he has heeded the call of night. I could tell that she did not admire my otherworldly looks; rather, she instantly assumed the worst — that I must be the masculine counterpart of Miriam the whore. She looked at me, and her dying son, and I could just imagine her thinking maybe I was the reason her Joshua could never settle down and have kids.

Then Joshua gasped, "Mother, he's your son now. John, kiss your new mother."

She gaped at the outrageous insinuation. I wanted to tell her it wasn't what she thought it was, but I daresay it would have made even less sense to her. Just like human beings, to stoop to a bit of domestic bickering at a moment like this.

I was surprised that he could still speak. The process of crucifixion is actually one of asphyxiation, of the body slowly sagging and collapsing the lungs. The power of speech soon goes.

"I'm thirsty," he said.

A small detail was marching uphill, pausing in front of each cross to smash the criminal's legs. Without the anchor of nailed-down bone, the body caves in on itself and squeezes the life right out of itself. Another practical Roman solution to the Jewish taboo about corpses being strung up past nightfall. No time to lose. I found a sentry, nodding off against a boulder. I shook him. "Let me give him something to drink," I said. I dropped a silver denarius in his helmet. He grunted, let me borrow his javelin for a moment; I pierced my left wrist with a fingernail and squeezed out enough blood to wet a sponge, held it up to his lips; blood trickled onto his tongue, which was already beginning to protrude.

When he tasted blood, something about him changed. Was it the touch of the first breath of eternity? Softly, he said, "It's done." But what was done? Surely not his crazed master plan for establishing the perfect Jewish society, god's kingdom on earth? Or was it an acceptance of his vampiric destiny? Only the night would tell.

He closed his eyes. The darkness gathered. But I left swiftly, for these unnatural darknesses have a way of lifting, and I did not want to be stranded in sunlight even on the short distance from the execution site to the tomb that Joseph of Arimathea had prepared — a luxurious tomb, for he had intended it for himself.

Once inside the tomb, I waited awhile; in time, my circadian rhythms, interrupted by the unnatural darkness of the afternoon, forced me back into slumber. I slept more than twenty-four hours; when I go out by day, even in darkness, my body needs a little longer to repair itself.

When I awoke, he was hunched on the lid of the stone sarcophagus, tearing the bloody linen off himself. "I'll get that," I said. I ripped away more pieces of his shroud. His wrists were regenerating nicely, but there was a deep puncture in each one, wide enough to stick a finger through.

"What did you do to me?" he said. "What have you made me?"

I said, "They begged me, your apostles. And I've seen it in your face. You want this. You've looked eternity in the eye before, Joshua, and it didn't scare you."

He didn't answer. He was staring at his hands. They were white as the limestone sepulcher itself. Yes, I knew he was no longer mortal. There was no source of light in the tomb, and yet he saw with the eyes of night; and for those who see as we see he himself was light, cold, phosphorescent, pale.

"This isn't what I had in mind, John," he said.

"Don't call me John anymore," I said, and instead cried out my own true name in the language of night, which only the dead can speak. In that instant he knew his true name, too, which cannot be spoken here.

I sensed his confusion, sensed also the incipient pangs of the great hunger; and slitting my wrist once more with my fingernail I gave him sustenance, becoming mother to him as well as midwife. He did not complain that the blood violated his dietary taboos; he knew already that to cross into our world is also to abandon the very concept of god. "I was hoping to be resurrected," he said. "But at the last minute I despaired; I tried to pray but all I could hear were the words of the psalmist about having been forsaken by god; that's true, isn't it? Instead of god, you came."

"And once you called me an angel."

"You still are. *Angelos:* messenger. But who sent you? That's what I can't figure out. Is this how we're going to defeat the Romans... by turning Judaea into a kingdom of the undead?"

"Just the sort of harebrained grand scheme you'd come up with. Get the long view, Joshua. You already have defeated the Romans. Do you know how old I am? I was old when the citadel of the Hittites was plundered and razed. Where are the Hittites now? A few scratches of cuneiform in other people's history books. Where are the Trojans now? The Minoans, the people of Thera, the Carthaginians? I've already defeated them, because I'm still here, remembering the taste of their blood, and they are dust. If you ask me a question, and I pause till the fall of Rome before I answer you, it is only a blink. The mortals cannot see the grand spectacle of their own lives; they cannot be as passionate as we, nor as pitiless. Don't you feel the thrill of it?"

"If you say so," he said.

But perhaps he didn't. I recalled the odor of his blood. The tranquility that had so intoxicated me... it had survived the transformation. Why had I been lecturing him about the sweep of history? He had felt all of that without even having experienced it, even as a mere mortal. It occurred to me that perhaps it was not my blood that had brought him back from the dead. Maybe he was some kind of natural vampire, self-creating, self-sufficient. I had never encountered anything like that, but if you think about it, there's got to have been at least one vampire to start the whole cycle off..

This was a disturbing line of thought. So I said, "Well, Joshua, if not for the sweep of history, then at least knowledge. We've spoken of India, but there are other lands too... Cathay ... there are some of us who have found a whole new continent to the west ... there are more worlds to conquer than your Roman Empire."

"And we shall conquer them, my friend," he said. He had freed himself from his winding-sheet now. He embraced me, and said, "We'll find new worlds and fresh philosophies."

"You mean it?" I said.

"You know that I can't lie," he said. Such is the loneliness of eternity that I welcomed what he said without considering its ambiguity.

Your Holiness and others ... I see that you are becoming heartily troubled by my narration. But it gets worse.

You all know the story of the empty tomb. We met up with the rest of the apostles at Joseph's, and a couple of other times. They all thanked me — somewhat perfunctorily, to be sure — for bringing Joshua back from the dead. Miriam and Joseph (the rabbi, not the tin tradesman) and the rest of that mixed-up brood went through a transformation of their own. Having shat on their wayward eldest all his life, they resolved to put him on a pedestal; the fat, spoiled little brother led the campaign to make Joshua's proto-Marxist precepts into the biggest new sect of Judaism.

A book of those down-home little parables and precepts was circulated underground — much like Chairman Mao's little red book — it's the "lost" book that biblical scholars — which many of you, reverend fathers, are not — call "Q". I know, it was a cheap trick, using xeroxed pages of my personal copy of "Q" to cause this, ah, ecumenical support group to be convened, and, yes, I will present you all with the entire manuscript after I've had my say — but how else was I going to get your reverend asses all in one room and to believe in the authenticity of my tale?

In any case, you'll find that the scholars were quite correct: virtually all of "Q" is quoted at length in the four canonical gospels. You won't find anything new in it. The scoop, Reverend Fathers (oh, I do apologize, Sister, I didn't notice you amongst all the male chauvinists) is in what I'm telling you. I know you're all spazzing already, but please hold your sphincters for just five more minutes.

Something really, really weird happened next: Christianity.

Joshua and I were gone for, oh, twenty years or so. It was wild and glorious ... the vampiric equivalent of a honeymoon. Yes, we went to India. We fed on pilgrims as they stripped to bathe in the Ganges. I did most of the hunting. Joshua saw the necessity of it, but was still queasy; he was still adjusting. We rode through jungles, were received by maharajahs, drank the blood of virgins, were venerated as gods in some cities, reviled as demons in others. Yes, we did set sail to what you now call America, so you Mormon elders may consider Mr. Joseph Smith's febrile imaginings, at least in part, vindicated. Joshua did not preach. Instead, he listened. He was like an empty vessel into which men poured what was best and worst in themselves. And I admired him for that, because in transcending mortality he had not lost compassion, which is usually the first thing to go. He grew in compassion, in fact. I had not known that was possible.

In time, we came back to the Levant, and it was in Ephesos, a town most famed for its huge gold statue of the Great Mother, that we first encountered Jesus Christ.

It was, in fact, in front of the famous statue (in Ephesos they call the mother-goddess Diana) that we first heard the name being bandied about. It was night and they were sacrificing — strange how that motif crops up again — and we were hunting. The place was a spectacle, all towering columns and clouds of incense and everything gold and ivory and the statue itself tall as a ten-story building. No babies being sacrificed here, though; we were well inside the civilizing boundaries of Rome. In the shadow of a fluted column, voices were whispering about Nazareth.

Joshua pricked up his ears. "They haven't forgotten me," he said, and smiled.

Good news. Baptism. The Kingdom of Heaven... the redemption of mankind ... the resurrection ... it sounded hauntingly familiar. There was a meeting later that night, we overheard. In a back room of a local synagogue.

The crowd was an odd one. I had never seen so many goyim in a synagogue, and they didn't cover their heads. There were women, too, sitting right alongside the men. A lot of riff-raff — slaves, the homeless, prostitutes — Joshua liked that. He had always gone down well with the proles, with that stuff about the first shall be last and blessed are the poor and camels going through needles' eyes and all that. One or two rich people, too. We blended right in; no one so much as stared at us.

The thing was as brilliantly stage-managed as a contemporary revival meeting. There were warm-up speakers, who gave testimonials about the efficacy of using the ineffable name of Jesus as a kind of mantra; Joshua chuckled a little at this, but as the meeting went on he became more and more solemn.

The keynote speaker was a man named Paul. Bit of a flamer, a Liberace type ... a real-live Roman citizen, as he never tired of pointing out. The tale he told was an amazing one, a sort of throw-it-in-the-blender mélange of every popular cult in the Roman Empire. Jesus was the son of God (like Hercules) and that bitter yenta of a mother was transformed into an eternal virgin, much like the Great Mother herself who was worshipped at the Temple of Diana down the street. Like Adonis, Jesus had died at the beginning of the spring fertility rites and been resurrected on the third day. Like Odin, he had been strung up on a great tree. Adam's dismissal from Eden was no longer what everyone had always thought it was, a profound, poetic metaphor for the human condition, but a temporary inconvenience to which Jesus would soon put an end, especially since he was coming back any moment now to snatch up the faithful and punish the sinful. The whole of the Tanakh was just Part One. All this was gospel truth because Paul, formerly Saul, had once persecuted Christians... and Jesus had come to him in a vision and set him straight.

Mixed in with all this fantasmagorical mythology were many of the homely parables and radical sociological viewpoints that Joshua had actually preached. It was very inspirational, very feverish, very much like a rock concert. Women were weeping and fainting and having orgasms; men were having attacks of glossolalia; cripples were tottering around and blind men claiming they could see while banging their heads on pillars.

As Paul's rhetoric climaxed with an appeal not to resist persecution _ to welcome martyrdom as it would mean instant acceptance into the bosom of Jesus. Crucifixion, flaying, burning, being devoured by lions, all were but painful preludes to paradise.

It got better. Next came a magic ritual _ a pagan parody of that sad last passover meal we had all had together, the night they came to take him away. They broke bread, and after a few incantations pronounced that it was Joshua's body; a flagon of wine became his blood. Such irony! It made me relive once more the moment I had first savored that blood, so innocent of inner turmoil. Eating the sacred body of the god-king was a custom as old as the Stone Age, but Paul had managed to trivialize even that most ancient and potent of metaphors. Fucking Roman citizen indeed. He certainly had their literal-mindedness.

"I can't take much more of this," I said, and we fought our way through the throng as someone bore down on us with a collection plate.

But suddenly Joshua stopped me. "We have to talk to him," he said. "This is insanity. We have to stop it."

"They're only humans," I said. "This will all blow over."

"But it's my name they're using," he said. "It's my name they're dying for."

"Your human name," I said scornfully.

"Yes," he said.

You know, we don't change all that much when we cross over to the darkness. Alive, Joshua had attracted me because he grasped eternity so completely; now that he was dead, I saw that his comprehension of mortality far surpassed my own. He had not been comfortable in their world, and now he had still not found his home.

I had to humor him. It was not in my power to douse this spark of difference in him; it was what I loved most about him.

Easy enough for us to blend into the shadows, to drift along the dusty columns until we found a back room, where a young man stood flexing in front of a polished shield. We stood behind this youth, too absorbed in his narcissistic endeavors to look over his shoulder — we cast no reflection in the shield, of course — and waited.

Presently we could hear a hymn being sung, fervently and discordantly, by the crowd outside, and Paul came storming into the room. We stepped back into gloom. Paul and the young man kissed passionately. "A strong showing tonight, Timothy," Paul said. "I think we've collected enough to hit the big time."

"You think we'll actually get to play Rome?" said the boy. The adoring gaze he had for the old man turned sour when Paul looked away, and I recognized the sullen mien of the street hustler. Definitely rough trade.

"Rome? Honey, we're going to own Rome!" said Paul.

Many theologians and sociologists have argued that St. Paul was a closet homosexual who imposed his misogyny on the misguided Christian masses; but let me tell you, Your Holiness — in spite of your recent encyclical — that civilized people in the first century were far too sophisticated to be hung up on such minutiae as sexual preference. Later, of course, when St. Augustine decided that sex was dirty....

We interrupted before the scene could become x-rated, materializing out of the shadows. "Paul!" Joshua said. "Do you know who I am?"

"No," he said, mystified. Timothy shrugged and went back to flexing.

Joshua held up his pierced wrists. You could see the smoky flicker of the wall torch through the holes.

"You're not," said Paul.

"I am," said Joshua barJoseph.

I stayed out of it. It was Joshua's fight. I lurked in the background. Outside, the hymn singing crescendoed to a cacophonous climax.

"Why are you doing this to me?" Joshua said softly.

"James and the others... they said you'd risen from the dead, said they'd seen it with my own eyes... thought it was the greatest new gimmick ... but it's true, then. Dear me, who would have thought it?"

Joshua said, "I'm not Dionysus. God didn't come down from heaven to screw my mother. I'm not Osiris, come back from the dead to guide mortals beyond the grave. I'm not the Corn God, ripped in pieces to fertilize the earth and then reborn as king. I'm just a rabbi who hung out with hookers. I wanted my friends to become better Jews, to understand what the Torah's really trying to say instead of hiding behind their petty regulations."

"What good are the Jews? They crucified you."

"No, they didn't. The Romans did."

"They made them do it."

"You don't make the Romans do things. I broke a Roman law. I would not render unto Caesar something which belonged to Caesar — sovereignty. I wasn't talking about political sovereignty, but you know how literal-minded the Romans are. Why would the Jews have had me killed? For claiming to be the messiah? There's a new messiah every week, and they don't get crucified."

I had to speak up. "He has to blame it on the Jews," I said. "He's preaching to the Romans. Roman complicity in your death would be a real no-no. What do the goyim know about the workings of the Sanhedrin? As far as they're concerned, a bunch of swarthy, middle-eastern religious fanatics is capable of any depravity... even Deicide. Have to bend the truth a bit here and there, don't you, Paul?"

"The truth! And what, as Pontius Pilate said to you, Jesus, on the morning of your crucifixion, is truth?"

"He didn't say that," said Joshua. "He didn't even talk to me. He had a dozen other death warrants to sign that morning, and he didn't want to miss lunch."

Paul was fuming. "You're just like your brother James," he said. "I've built this majestic structure of powerful, rich images that trigger the imagination, that make men's spirits soar. I'm giving hope to the downtrodden and picking up a few denarii along the way. So what if it's a house of cards? So what if it didn't really happen that way? I've found the core of mythic truth in your tawdry little bio, and I'm going to make you the biggest thing since the invention of the wheel, you ungrateful insect. This new religion is going to take over the world. It's got everything. Tragedy and pathos, terror of judgment, the catharsis of forgiveness. It's the grandest religion yet invented."

"But I don't want a new religion," said Joshua barJoseph. "I'm Jewish."

—

After a while, Paul seemed to calm down a little. "I'll need to regroup a little," he said. "Maybe I can still salvage some of this."

While he guzzled wine, we told him some of our own adventures. We got drunk together... he and Timothy on a couple of kegs of Samian wine, Joshua and I from a pint of Timothy's blood which he obligingly let me draw... after I told him I could do it painlessly.

Paul became so drunk he even stopped speaking Greek. In tearful Aramaic, he told us searing childhood tales about his father whipping him for sucking off the stablehands. No wonder he preferred being Roman to being Jewish! No wonder he wanted to bring the gospel to the goyim!

That was what it all boiled down to after all. He wanted to be accepted, to be loved for what he was, this poor little sissy boy who had the misfortune to be born into the one culture where they stoned sissies. One could almost sympathize. After a while, indeed, one did. "Forgive me," Paul was weeping into his goblet.

"I forgive you," said Joshua.

"Thank you... thank you, abba," said Paul. I realized then that he wanted his real father to forgive him... that the source of the angst that drove him was his fear of having disappointed his earthly father... he had created in his mind a surrogate father, all-merciful, all-forgiving, to succour his own self-loathing. And Joshua understood all this... truly understood it... and felt compassion for this lonely little man... a compassion as deep as any love he felt for me.

I envied the world, because not even death had sundered Joshua from his love for it.

Paul invited us back to his home. "I want to hear more stories," he said. "I want to learn everything you can teach me. After all, you are my redeemer. You ought to have a hand in the religion, especially since it's all about you."

Very softly, Joshua said to me, "He just doesn't hear me."

But we went home with him anyway, and as dawn approached we bedded down for the day in a cosy wine-cellar.

Night fell and I rose from my dreamless sleep. I found my beloved disciple lying on the dirt floor, unmoving, in a pool of still, cold blood, with a stake through his heart.

Paul and Timothy had gone on to Rome.

And I too fled, for the inchoate feelings that raged through me were too much like my memories of pain.

He must have known. He had a sense about such things. He must have realized that Paul could not long abide the shattering of his great glass cathedral with the hammer of blunt reality.

He loved the world. He loved beautiful things, cities, trees, animals, and even more so, people. It must have pained him more than I can imagine, to choose to leave the world behind. Why, then? Was it that he could not face the prospect of his name being taken in vain by thousands, thousands who would become millions, billions? Did he sense that his homespun stories about shepherds and widow's mites and mustard seeds would become the official religion of the Roman empire, that that religion would plunge the western world into a Dark Age for a thousand years, that it would spawn senseless massacres, enslavements of entire peoples, wanton destructions of countless noble, ancient, beautiful cultures?

I don't know.

Your Holiness, Reverend Fathers, Your Eminence, and ... yes, Reverend Sister ... this is what I know.

He was good. I have never known anyone before or since who has truly deserved that adjective. He was brilliant. He loved, deeply and with complete commitment. He possessed an absolute empathy even for the dispossessed. These qualities were in his very blood.

The blood of mortals is spiced with the hormones of desire and fear, but his was not. It was to other blood as a sparkling mountain stream is to the murky effluvium of a city faucet. It was the Platonic absolute of blood. It was pure. It was the holy grail of bloods, the true taste of which all other tastes are but an echo.

We are much alike, you who have hocus-pocused a million gallons of cheap wine and call it redemption, and I who have savored your savior's actual blood. We cannot believe he is gone forever. Love such as ours, we desperately think, cannot stay unrequited for ever. The Absolute is by its very nature Eternal.

We live — you for a few heartbeats, I for all time — in the hope (the fear, too) that he will come again. He must come again.

The river of time is long. I know. Trust me. One day he will. Suddenly. Without warning.

Like a vampire in the night.

About the Author ❧

Called by the International Herald Tribune "the most well-known expatriate Thai in the world," Somtow Sucharitkul (S.P. Somtow) is a composer, author and media personality whose talents have entertained fans the world over.

Born in Thailand, Somtow grew up in several European countries and was educated at Eton and Cambridge. His first career was in music. His 1975 composition "Views from the Golden Mountain" was the first to combine Thai and Western instruments into new sonorities. In the 1970s, Somtow established himself as a prominent Southeast Asian avant-garde composer, causing considerable controversy in his native country as artistic director of the Asian Composers Expo 78. He founded the Thai Composers' Association, and was the permanent representative of Thailand to the International Music Council of UNESCO.

A severe case of musical burnout caused Somtow to turn to writing in the early 1980s, and he soon produced a succession of over forty books in several genres under the pen name S.P. Somtow, winning numerous awards for such novels as "Vampire Junction" (Gollancz), today considered a classic of gothic literature and taught in "gothic lit" courses around the U.S.A. His semi-autobiographical memoir "Jasmine Nights," published by Hamish Hamilton, prompted George Axelrod, Oscar-winning writer of "Breakfast at Tiffany's", to refer to him as "the J.D. Salinger of Siam." He has just finished a stint as president of the Horror Writers' Association. His most recent books are "Tagging the Moon — Fairy Tales of Los Angeles" and "Dragon's Fin Soup." His novels have been translated into about a dozen languages. He also dabbled in filmmaking, directing a couple of low-budget films during his years in Los Angeles. 1990s, he began to turn back to music, rejecting his previous embrace of the musical fashions of the 60s and 70s and reinventing himself as a neo-Romantic composer. His recent works include the ballet "Kaki" and the "Mahajanaka Symphony" composed for the King of Thailand's 72nd birthday.

In 1999, he was commissioned to compose what turned out to be the first opera by a Thai composer ever to be premiered, "Madana", inspired by a fairytale-like play written by King Rama VI of Siam and dedicated to his wife, Queen Indrasaksachi, who was also the composer's great-aunt. For this opera, he has chosen to compose in the late-Romantic idiom that would have been familiar to his great-aunt and her royal spouse, with a liberal garnish of Southeast Asian sonorities. The opera premiered in February 2001 in Bangkok in what was called, by *Opera Now* magazine, "one of the operatic events of the year."

Somtow's second opera on a Thai theme, *Mae Naak,* opened on January 6, 2003 in Bangkok. He has just won the World Fantasy Award, the most coveted writing award in the field of fantasy literature, for his short story "The Bird Catcher." He commutes between his two homes in Los Angeles and Bangkok.

In the second half of 2003, Somtow conducted the Thailand premiere of the Brahms Requiem as part of a 100-concert-worldwide memorial to Daniel Pearl, and presented an evening of Wagner in honour of Wolfgang Wagner. He also directed a production of "The Turn of the Screw." Japanese director Takashi Miike is adapting his award-nominated story "Dragon's Fin Soup" into a French-produced feature film and hid novel, *Vampire Junction,* is being adapted into an opera by French composer Frédéric Chaslin.

Currently he is artistic director of the Bangkok Opera, Siam Philharmonic and Orpheus Choir of Bangkok.

www.ingramcontent.com/pod-product-compliance
Lightning Source LLC
Chambersburg PA
CBHW030824310726
48980CB00006B/627/J

* 9 7 8 0 9 7 7 1 3 4 6 8 7 *